THINGS COME

COME

Together 2

Darrius Williams

Published by TJS Publishing House
www.tjspublishinghouse.com
contact@tjspublishinghouse.com

Published in the United States of America

ISBN-13: 978-1-952833-32-8
ISBN-10: 1-952833-32-9

Table of Contents

CHAPTER 1

Dallas, TEXAS

Berry Residence

A strong heaviness accompanied by what felt like a heat wave came over the room. There were very few moments that Derek could remember feeling such thick tension in a room. Katie stood frozen as she stared at her father's brooding figure at the end of the hallway. Her little sister Olivia broke the tension, running full speed towards Katie and jumping into her arms. Olivia's arms wrapped tightly around Katie's neck.

"You are more beautiful every time I see you," Katie said to her.

Katie knew all eyes were on the two of them but was in no rush to engage with everyone else, especially her father. She stood up to see her mother standing beside her father, smiling as she watched her two daughters embrace. Her father Walter's tall and broad frame was imposing, and his strong cheekbones aided in his stone-cold stares. Katie reached over and locked arms with Derek, walking him down towards her parents as if the two of them were walking down the aisle.

"Dad," Katie said quietly, forcing herself to smile.

Walter did not say a word; he stared at Katie intensely as Katie's forced smile began to fade. Her heart then began to race. The silence in the room felt amplified.

"It's good to see you," she then said.

Derek glanced over at Katie, assuming that Walter was simply giving her a hard time. Walter and Laura suddenly turned and looked at one another, then burst into laughter, breaking up the tension. Katie let out a nervous laugh also as Walter's long arms pulled her in for a tight hug. The last place Katie expected to be, was in the arms of her father. She felt as if she was hugging a distant relative.

"It's good to see you beautiful," Walter said. "I've missed you."

After they separated, the two of them looked into each other's eyes. Walter had a way of making people feel as if he was staring into their soul when he looked at them. He had much more grey hair than Katie remembered, and his skin was a little more weathered than she remembered. Katie stepped back and turned towards Derek.

"Dad, this is Derek."

"Nice to meet you," Derek extended his hand towards Walter.

Walter took a slightly deep breath, then reached out and shook Derek's hand. The loud sound of their hands slapping against each other echoed through the hallway.

"How's it going," Walter said in his delayed response.

"I appreciate you having me Mr. Berry."

"You enjoy the flight?" Walter quickly asked him.

"It was cool, slept through most of it, my mouth probably was wide open," Derek chuckled as he looked at Katie.

For Katie, the whole exchange was awkward and forced, and one that she hoped would just be quick and easy. Walter simply kept nodding despite the brief laughs; he didn't crack a smile as he continued staring at Derek.

"Taking care of my daughter?"

"Yes sir, most definitely."

"Oh okay," Walter nodded as if impressed with Derek's answer. "She taking care of you?"

"She's good to me, most definitely."

Derek thought it was simple innocent interaction between the two of them, but Katie knew her father all too well. She did not like where the conversation was going.

"Let me show you where you can put your things," Katie grabbed Derek's attention.

"Yeah go on and show him," Walter pat Derek on the back.

"If you need the lac you can use it, in case you don't want to be stuck in this big palace of a house," Robert said sarcastically.

"Thanks pa, I might drive him around. We'll see," Katie threw her bag over her shoulder.

"Too bad we aren't in Houston, you could have shown Derek all of your old stomping grounds," Glenda said as she read an article on her phone.

"Well, Galveston isn't that far, they can if they want this weekend," Laura said.

Katie escorted Derek through a door in the kitchen that led to another part of the house. She was glad to be out of the spotlight of attention. It was surreal for her to walk through the house that she hadn't been to in years.

"This house is crazy," Derek said as they walked into the guest bedroom.

"It's alright," Katie said. "Nothing special."

"I thought I was going to be in a basement, whew," Derek jokingly wiped his forehead.

"Ha-ha, you're in luck, we don't have a basement," Katie threw down her book bag.

The bedroom was plain, no major decorations, just a large queen-sized bed, a nightstand, and a forty-inch flat-screen television mounted on the wall. Despite it being a guest room, it was quite spacious and comfortable. Katie still had a wave of anxiety on the inside but felt herself getting more comfortable as time went on. She still was not as comfortable as she wanted to be. Despite being home, she did not feel at home.

"Aye," a voice made them turn towards the door.

"Oh my God!" Katie walked over quickly and hugged her younger brother Jared Berry, taken aback by how much Jared had grown in such a short period of time.

"Boy I just saw you a few years ago!"

Jared was a few inches taller than Katie, his high-top fade with a design cut into the back of his head gave him a few more inches. He also had a much deeper voice and was a little more muscular than Katie remembered. The last time she saw Jared, he was shorter, scrawny, and he always looked like a little boy despite his age.

"Why are you so sweaty?" Katie asked as she pulled lent out of Jared's hair.

"Relax," he moved her hand, excited to see his sister.

It was clear to Derek that Jared played basketball from the sweaty tank top he had on along with the shorts, high socks, and flip-flops.

"You hoop?" he asked Jared.

"Yeah, do you?" Jared's eyes lit up.

Katie removed herself from the conversation and pulled out her phone. As Jared and Derek talked about basketball, she sat on the bed looking through the text messages from her friends Sabrina, Paris, and Imani. Laura then appeared in the doorway.

"I'm making dinner tonight; do you want to go to the store for me while you're out?" she asked Katie.

"I mean, you already sent me a grocery list so…" Katie smiled and held up her phone.

Laura then looked over at Derek.

"This is enough room for you huh?" she said sarcastically.

"More than enough."

Laura looked at Katie, then back at Derek, and back at Katie again. She then sighed with a smile on her face before walking out. Katie and Derek looked at each other smiling.

"She likes you," Katie told him, eyebrows raised. "Already getting in good."

"She is really nice," Derek replied.

"And Jared," Laura's voice came from down the hall. "Don't sit around and haven't showered, make sure you get in that shower and don't be walking around here nasty!"

Jared shook his head with a frown on his face as he walked out.

"Oh, she can turn up," Derek chuckled as Katie nodded.

Katie was not surprised that her mother liked Derek, anyone with sense could see that he was a good man and there wasn't anything not to like. She just hoped and prayed that her father had a least a spec of that sense.

CHAPTER 2

A change of scenery and some time away from the day-to-day routine were two things that Derek and Katie didn't realize they needed. Riding around Dallas in Laura's white Range Rover before making their way to the grocery store provided just that. It didn't take much time in Dallas for Derek to truly realize how well Katie had it growing up and the means that were available to her. She rarely talked about it and often downplayed it, but seeing it in person made it impossible to deny. Derek was comfortable and relaxed, guards completely down. He still did not understand why Katie was a nervous wreck that whole morning, he felt nothing but positive energy and love thus far.

"This Range is clean!" Derek yelled over the loud music, causing Katie to quickly turn it down so that she could hear him.

"I want her to let me take this off of her hands, but she not hearing ya' girl," Katie said.

"I'd be mad at her if she did let you take this back to Charlotte."

"Yeah okay, you'd be flexing in it though," she fired back at him.

Once they returned from the grocery store, Derek carried all the bags in as Katie walked aimlessly in front of him.

"Thank you, Derek," Laura walked outside. "Such a gentleman, don't let Miss Hollywood work you like a slave."

"What? Work him like a...girl please!" Katie pulled her sunglasses off.

Derek carried the rest of the grocery bags into the kitchen. Katie sat on the couch and turned on the TV.

"Umm no ma'am," Laura said before walking into the kitchen. "You are about to help me cook, so let's rock and roll."

Katie's mouth dropped. Derek enjoyed seeing them go back and forth.

"Yo," Jared appeared, basketball in hand. "Still trying to play?"

"Yeah, let me help your mom--"

"No, go on. You've done enough. She will take it from here," Laura said, grinning at Katie.

Derek changed into some shorts and basketball shoes that he brought with him. Katie stood and watched Jared and Derek for a few minutes after she moved Laura's truck to clear the driveway. After a few minutes of shooting around and small talk, the two of them began to play against each other and compete hard against each other. Jared was quick and had great handles, but most of all he was a very good shooter. While Derek was impressed, Jared was even more impressed with all that Derek could do.

"You could get a free ride easily, a lot of college players can't hoop like you can already," Derek told him.

"We'll see, I'm trying to go to a big school."

Jared reminded Derek of himself at that age, from basketball, the mellow attitude, and wanting to play at a big school. Just from the few hours of playing, Derek became a big fan of Jared and truly respected his game.

"Your pops used to play or something? How you get cold like this?" Derek asked.

His question caused Jared to frown and shake his head as he dribbled. Jared drove past Derek, who leaped up and blocked Jared's layup attempt. The loud sound of his hand slapping against the basketball made it that much more impactful.

"He definitely didn't play, he's only seen me play like twice, and that's when I was little. He ain' been to a game in years. He doesn't care, honestly."

"For real?"

Jared shot the ball, completely missing it.

"I stopped talking to him about it. He in his own world a lot of times, so I just do me."

Derek struggled to wrap his mind around what Jared said, it was the last thing he expected to hear. Their family seemed so close in Derek's eyes.

"I'm not trying to make you think he a bad dude or anything," Jared said. "You just meeting him so—"

"Nah you good bro. So y'all never talk about it?"

"Nothing to talk about. When his mind is made up, that's it. He focused on what he wanna' do and it's his way or the highway. If you don't line up with what he wants to do, you just wallpaper to him. I mean look at how his situation with my sister is, and that's his firstborn."

Derek's eyes widened.

"Hold up, what situat—"

"Hey ashy!" Katie yelled from the front door, grabbing their attention. "Both of y'all looked up, that is too funny. Dinner is about to be done so wrap it up."

It began to get dark by the time Katie came outside. As Jared and Derek walked through the garage, his mind was stuck on what Jared said to end their game. He began to wonder what the situation was between Katie and Walter, and more importantly, why he had no idea what Jared was referring to...

CHAPTER 3

In the Berry home, eating dinner as a family was a regular occurrence. Even when Walter was away on business or working late, Laura and the kids all ate dinner together. There was a long dark brown wooden table in the dining room where dinner was served. The sight of everyone around a long table for family dinner was refreshing for Derek, it was something that he wanted for his own family someday. Walter sat at the head of the table along with Laura to the right, sitting closely to him. Tristan sat right beside Laura so that she could assist him with his food and his plate. Robert and Glenda were the next two beside Laura. On Walter's left sat Katie and Derek, then Jared and Olivia.

The main dish was homemade lasagna that everyone passed around in a glass dish to get their portion. In a separate bowl, there was a salad put together that was also passed around, in addition to a long silver tray with large pieces of garlic bread for everyone to partake in. Katie continued to grab Derek's hand or lock her arm with his. She continued to have side conversations with him despite

13

everything happening around them. While listening to Katie, Derek continued to catch Walter's glance at the two of them sharply every time they embraced or spoke to one another. He tried not to continue to catch eye contact with Walter, but he could not help it. Walter would stare intently.

The first half of dinner was full of discussion about various topics and many laughs. In most of the discussions, Laura spoke the most in depth and had several teaching moments. She was very knowledgeable in many different areas and could confidently articulate that which she knew, especially history.

"She thinks she's in the classroom still," Jared said.

"Oh I don't have to be in the classroom to teach y'all something baby," Laura smiled as Glenda and Katie gassed her up.

"You're a teacher?" Derek asked.

"She was," Walter answered, causing Derek to quickly look over at him.

Walter's strong voice easily demanded the attention of a room when he spoke, just as his presence did.

"She taught for a while at the high school and college level," he said as he and Laura smiled at one another.

"Wow," Derek nodded.

Katie grabbed Derek's hand under the table again, this time holding it tight.

"Do you remember when you got into that heated debate at the dinner table a while back about education?" Walter asked Laura. "Who was that? Isaac? That tried to debate you that time?"

An awkward silence quickly came across the table.

"What? No," Laura quickly dismissed it with a forced grin on her face.

Katie looking like a deer in headlights made it evident that she was caught off guard by Walter's question. Laura's frowning at Walter, Jared's widened eyes, and a few other reactions around the table were an indication that Katie wasn't the only one. The moment did not pass as quickly as Laura would have liked. Katie's phone beginning to vibrate and light up saved everyone from the awkward moment. She reached out in front of her plate and grabbed it, relieved.

"Is your phone going off?" she then asked Derek.

Derek did not respond, still glancing over at Walter. Katie's eyes suddenly widened.

"Oh my God, what?" Katie said aloud as she began to viciously type a text.

Everyone's eyes were now fixed on her.

"What's going on?" Walter asked.

Katie ran into the family room, followed by Olivia.

"Honey, what are you looking for?" Glenda asked, also following her into the family room.

After flipping through several channels, Katie stopped on one of the news channels. The screen was split between the news anchor and live footage of several large groups in Charlotte screaming, chanting, and being restrained by SWAT teams.

"…as you can see to my left, massive crowds and outrage tonight in Charlotte, just awful. We hope everyone is remaining safe, we're already aware of several bystanders injured by bottles thrown and other objects. No full story has emerged regarding Johnson's shooting; police say that Johnson as well as another assailant fled the scene and that is when police opened fire after commanding the men several times to stop and surrender their weapons. Both are believed to have been armed and extremely dangerous as— "

"Oh my God," Katie stared, eyes wide in disbelief.

"Katie what happened?" Olivia asked, glued to Katie's hip.

"Hold on O," Katie put her arm around Olivia, still focused on the TV as others made their way into the family room.

Derek recognized the mug shots that appeared on the screen during the news report. One of the two he used to see linger around campus back in college, the other he remembered having a class or two with. Katie began to explain to her grandparents that she knew the two on the screen and how. Tavares Kingston and his older cousin, Andre Burrell, were both shot by the police. Andre survived, Tavares did not, and the city of Charlotte was in an uproar about the situation. Katie, in disbelief, left the family room to call someone.

"So sad…" Laura shook her head.

Walter was the last one to walk into the family room, not paying any mind to the news.

"Going to do some work, be up in a second," he said to Laura.

"Not too late, you need rest too," Laura said.

Walter leaned down and kissed her forehead, he then walked past Derek without acknowledging or making eye contact with him. Derek stared him down as he walked past, feeling the slight sense of tension between the two of them. The tension began to come across to Derek as disrespect, which he did not like. Katie walked back in and wrapped her arms around Derek.

"Come on, I'll take you to your room."

Katie walked Derek back to the guest room, her arms still wrapped around him as they walked side by side.

"You alright?" he asked.

"I'm worried," she said. "I'm worried about Miah. She didn't answer my calls. You know Tavares is Deron's daddy."

"That's where I know them from!"

"Yeah boy," she softly slapped his face. "You know you used to listen to the tea."

Derek sat down on the bed, taking off his shoes and getting comfortable.

"I just can't believe it, man," Katie shook her head. "They killed that boy."

"It's crazy," Derek said, unsure of what else to say.

"And Paris and 'dem are texting me about it. I just don't need them to say anything that's gon' set me off."

"About somebody getting killed?"

"Yeah, messed up right? But you know Tavares is the reason they treat Miah the way they do…that's a whole different story I don't feel like getting into right now," Katie said as she finally stopped texting. "Well, goodnight. Long day tomorrow."

"Hold up," Derek grabbed her arm, stopping her from walking out and stood in front of her. "Why you trying to leave so fast?"

"Sorry, I'm just a little tired," Katie said as she rubbed her eyes, then carelessly looked up at Derek. "I wasn't trying to be short. Are you enjoying yourself? Everyone treating you right?"

"Yeah, your family is cool. Your daddy acting like he got some things on his mind."

Katie shook her head. Derek mentioned it in hopes of sparking further conversation; he was anxious to ask about Jared's comment from their basketball game earlier that night.

"That's just how he is. He is not the most social person."

"Your brother said he acts standoffish too," Derek said, causing Katie to pause and glance over at him.

"Who said that? Jared?"

"Yeah, he said that outside."

Derek waited to see if he would get somewhere, but Katie went from deep thought to a shrug and being unbothered again. She gave Derek a quick kiss then left out of the room. Derek laid back, then quickly sat up after feeling something uncomfortable poke him in his back. As he felt around the bed for what poked him, he heard something fall on the side of the bed. It turned out to be a small navy-blue leather book with a red ribbon coming out of it. When he picked it up, a picture fell out of it. His eyes widened when he saw the picture, it was an old college picture of Katie and Isaac on the Darcy campus. Although the picture was old, he found himself frowning at it with his heart speeding up a little. He opened the blue book and recognized Katie's handwriting. He laid back in the bed and began to read, not sure what he would uncover.

CHAPTER 4

Two small lamps in the middle of the family room saved it from being in total darkness. Well after midnight, Katie and Laura sat facing each other on the couch, drinking one of Laura's favorite margarita drink concoctions. After Katie tucked Olivia in and put her to bed, she came back to the family room to talk with her mother for what had been hours. She admired Laura not just as her mother, but also as a woman.

"You made Derek stay in that guest room all by himself, leaving that man lonely?"

"Please," Katie rolled her eyes. "That would have happened regardless; we stopped sleeping in the same bed."

Laura's eyes widened as she slowly lowered her drink glass from her mouth.

"So, you two don't spend the night with each other?"

"We used to but stopped. Too many close calls," Katie took a sip of her drink.

"Yeah you probably are really fertile just like your mama."

"I'm not talking about pregnancy, I'm talking about doing the do," Katie laughed.

"So," Laura leaned in, whispering. "You two aren't…"

"No, trying to wait," Katie stood and walked over toward the piano.

On top of the piano was a tray with three wine bottles and other alcohol, along with drink glasses on it. Katie poured herself more of the drink that Laura made.

"That is admirable… and so rare," Laura said, amazed.

Laura made people comfortable being transparent. She was easy to speak with, but the boundary of her being a mother was never blurred.

"How long have you been doing that?"

"It's been like three years now, remember I told you?"

"I remember us talking about you going to that church up there in New York and you really liked it. You were getting more in tune with your spiritual side… Is that why you two, you know…" Laura began to gesture again, causing Katie to roll her eyes.

"Lord ma, haven't had sex? Yes, that's why," Katie smiled.

"I don't know why I thought pregnancy," Laura chuckled.

"I know why, because of what happened with you know who," Katie said. "I won't say his name because it's been said enough tonight."

Laura silently laughed, grabbing Katie's hand leaning into her.

"Girl I almost fell out of my chair!" Laura kept trying not to laugh too loud as Katie just rolled her eyes, trying to keep from laughing herself.

"Anyway, I almost forgot about the situation with him. I haven't thought about it since then. You talked about being abstinent then too, that's what I thought you were going to say. It's something to laugh at now," Laura said.

"Yeah, *now* it is," Katie settled her feet under her on the couch. "I was scared for my life. Did you ever tell—"

"No, no, no. There was nothing to tell."

"But you know how he is, he would have torn this whole house apart."

"I know all too well."

Laura stared at her daughter. She was so happy to have Katie home, some moments she would just stare at her beautiful daughter and admire how much she'd grown. Katie analyzed the living room as if she was a guest, observing everything. She did not have many memories there, having only stayed there during holiday breaks when she was in college. Despite how beautiful the house was, she preferred their old home in Houston.

"You know, I loved seeing the two of you hug today. It really felt good seeing that again you just don't know."

"Yeah," Katie said. "I really missed the kiddos. They are growing up like crazy, got me feeling old."

As the conversation began to turn toward serious matters, small awkward silences became more prevalent.

"Why did you stay away so long?" Laura's question caused them to lock eyes. "Why were you so determined to?"

Katie looked away from Laura, caught off guard.

"I wasn't trying to, you know… life happens, sometimes time just sneaks by you."

Laura continued to stare at Katie, completely unconvinced.

"You truly are your father's child," Laura took a sip. "I know you, and I know it has something to do with him."

Katie laid back and let out a deep sigh.

"He did a good job of driving me away, boxing me out, and then there you were, always sticking by him, always caping for him."

"He's my husband."

"I'm your daughter," Katie snapped back and quickly sat up.

"I am not going to let you make this about choosing sides," Laura said strongly. "We are not on opposite sides. We are a family. Enough is enough."

"Well I guess that is why I am here," Katie said sarcastically. "Trying to be the bigger person and extend myself first even though I shouldn't."

"Even though you shouldn't?"

"Even though I shouldn't."

"So that's why you're here? Thank God," Laura rolled her eyes in sarcasm.

"Don't be like that," Katie frowned.

"It seems like you came here to show that you have Derek and to show JR in a 'stick it to him' kind of way," Laura caused Katie's look of confusion to intensify.

"That is... wow... I assure you, that's not something that even crossed my mind. I had to fight myself to even get here, not that I didn't want to see y'all. I love y'all. But, after all that we've fought about and the constant back and forth... it's just been a never-ending battle with him."

"I know," Laura said.

Katie let out a light laugh that broke up the tension.

"What are you laughing at?"

"How do you put up with it? You are actually married to the man and have to share a bed with him," Katie caused them both to laugh.

"Your dad wasn't always how he is now, he's just... I don't know. He's been a little down on himself and just has some things he needs to deal with on his own. I try to pinpoint it, but he's stubborn like you," Laura said.

"Really?" Katie's smile faded.

"Just being honest. But despite how frustrating it can be and times where we have our own wars with each other, I still ride for him to the end. He's my best friend, I'm always going to fight for him, even when it seems like the whole world is against him."

Katie slowly nodded, carefully choosing her words. It sounded great, but she did not care to hear that regarding her father.

"Can you say that about Derek?" Laura asked.

"Say what?"

"Is he a man you can follow and trust?"

"Oh," Katie said, feeling uneasy. "I would say so; I think I can."

"You need to do better than 'I think'."

Laura stood up and walked over to the large television.

"I mean, I actually do trust him. That is how I know he is different because I can actually trust him and let my guards down. It's just hard letting go and embracing that."

"I get it."

"Men are just dumb," Katie caused them both to burst out into laughter. "They can be so dumb sometimes!"

"*Some*times?"

Laura turned on the television to a random sitcom, turning the volume up just enough to where they could hear each other yet difficult for a person to eavesdrop.

"But seriously, they need us to be there for them, and keep reminding them that they're more than capable of leading and being what we need, what society needs more of. Things change when men are doing what they are supposed to do, and them being in their rightful place only benefits us."

It was easy for a person to see how Laura used to teach, her voice and the way she spoke was very engaging.

"So, it is important that you can stand by him, which is why I asked. You can't stand by a man and belittle him at the same time."

"You're right, you are right."

There was not much else that needed to be said, nor anything for her to add. Katie honestly was tired of talking about everything that she was blitzed about over the past week, her dad, marriage, relationship, she just wanted to stop it from being the focal point of everything.

"I've talked your ear off long enough I'm sure," Laura interrupted Katie's thoughts.

"No, no I love talking to you. You know, woman to woman." Katie flashed a smile.

Laura gave Katie a long hug.

"I love you so much."

"I love you too," Katie said before heading toward the stairs.

"Oh!" Laura suddenly yelled, "I told you I found that blue journal, right?"

Katie jolted.

"Where is it?"

"I don't know. I had it, and then it disappeared. I meant to give it to you when you got here."

"Wow," Katie said. "I'd burn it if I had it."

"That bad? I kept your dad from reading it, that's as bad as it could get right?"

"Pretty much," Katie said with a shrug. "I mean... other than Derek reading it."

CHAPTER 5

Charlotte, NORTH CAROLINA

Two years prior...

The pouring rain and ugly dark sky ironically provided the soothing feeling that Katie needed to put her at ease. She remained planted on her couch watching some of her favorite sitcoms from the nineties, which put her in a much better mood. She always watched old sitcoms, laughing each time as if it was her first time seeing them. It took her most of the day, but she'd finally began to find some peace despite all that happened. Katie checked her phone for the first time since talking to Laura earlier, surprised that she didn't have any missed calls or texts. Within a few minutes of her phone being in her hand, the name SOPHIA BARLOW flashed across her screen. Sophia graduated from Darcy with Katie and her friends but was someone that Katie rarely spoke with. When Katie answered, Sabrina's voice was the one that came from the other end.

"Girl, you need to get down here right now!" Sabrina yelled over all the noise in the background.

"Sabrina? What you got going on?"

"Get down here. Your man is in here acting a fool, you need to come down here," Sabrina urged her over the phone.

"What?" Katie asked in confusion. "He doesn't even go to clubs, you sure it's him?"

"I am positive!" Sabrina yelled.

The noise suddenly toned down in the background, enabling Katie to hear Sabrina better.

"I just stepped into the bathroom, I'm using Fe's phone, my phone is trippin'. But girl, please come down here. He is not looking good right now."

Concern gripped Katie as she listened to Sabrina over the phone, but it was followed up with anger from the fact that Derek had ignored her all night long. Was she supposed to go save him? Her frustrations began to get the better of her.

"He's with his friends I'm sure, and he's grown, he can take care of himself."

"Katie are you serious? You really not coming?" Sabrina asked frantically.

"No."

When the two of them got off the phone, Katie sat her phone on the table and lay back down on the couch. She did well not to think about Derek and being at peace; but that tranquility ended abruptly. Despite returning to her shows, Katie continued to glance at her phone every couple of seconds.

"I just need to go to bed," she said aloud to herself.

Twenty minutes later, her phone vibrated with a notification just as she had expected. When she picked the phone up this time, Sabrina's name showed up on her screen. Katie opened her messages to see that she was sent a video. In the video, Derek was being sat down on one of the couches in the section that he was in. Katie recognized Derek's friends, Tone and Trent, who both stood in front of Derek. She realized that the two of them were calming Derek down, who had a scowl on his face. Derek then made a staggering, yet swift dart towards someone, again being grabbed by Tone and Trent.

"What the hell?" she asked aloud as if Derek could hear her.

When Derek was sat down, a woman then appeared and wrapped her arm around him, calming him down. The woman then sat on Derek's lap, caressing his face and neck. She was in a tight black dress, having to adjust it every time she sat or even shifted, to avoid showing too much. Katie's temper suddenly rose to a boil. She immediately recognized the woman, which caused her temper to flare even further. Katie got up, put on her gym shoes, sweatpants and a jacket, grabbed her keys, and rushed out to her Jeep. *Why am I doing this? Why? Idiot!* A part of her felt like a fool thinking about how Derek ignored her for most of the day.

The rain showered down stronger as the night went on, yet Katie's driving took neither the wetness of the road or darkness into consideration. She was solely focused on getting to Derek, swerving between lanes and driving around cars full speed. Other drivers blew at her because of how risky she drove, hood over her head and her music loud as usual. Even with the music being as loud as it was, her thoughts echoed in her mind even louder. *I really feel like this about him. I look crazy. Maybe I AM crazy.*

When she pulled up to the club, there was a small line of people at the door waiting to get in. The rain stopped by the time she arrived but many of the people in line were soaked from getting caught in it. Sabrina met Katie outside, bracing herself while walking as if trying to keep her balance. She was in a short sequin dress and some heels that made her look much taller than she was. Sabrina was always able to get away with wearing certain clothes without showing too much because of her small frame.

"Drunk?" Katie asked, taking off her jacket and throwing it in her Jeep.

"Girl no, these heels are killing me," Sabrina let out a sigh of relief when she leaned against Katie's Jeep and took her heels off. "You got some flats in here?"

"Like you could fit them with those big feet!" Katie turned dramatically to Sabrina.

"We wear the same size hoe," Sabrina said, making Katie laugh.

After she handed Sabrina a pair of her flats, Katie then set her eyes on the club. Sabrina quickly followed her as she walked towards the doors with no hesitation. Neither of them had any intention of waiting in line or being charged to go in. The bouncer at the door was no shorter than six foot five and was a solid muscular man, ready to showcase his strength the moment someone got out of line. He recognized Sabrina since she was already inside, but then glanced over at Katie and crossed his arms.

"I need to bring her in with me, she only coming in to get somebody," Sabrina said. "I promise, she is not staying."

"They can meet her outside," the bouncer said.

"No, he can barely walk. She gotta' go in and get—"

"Not letting her in, she not even in the dress code," the bouncer cut Sabrina off.

"I have seen y'all let people in here with much worse on. I can't go in just to get somebody out?" Katie asked.

The irritation in her voice caused the bouncer to step closer to her, peering down at her as if threatening her. His goal was to intimidate her as he stared her down, but Katie did not budge.

"Did you not hear what I said to you? What part are you missing?" he asked aggressively.

"I heard everything you said. Maybe you don't get what *I* am saying—"

"Step out of line! Not about to go back and forth! Now."

As Katie began to verbally snap back at the bouncer, a man suddenly jumped in between the two of them. He was one of the founders of the promotion group that was hosting the party, Mack Vaughn. Katie recognized him from being around Darcy's campus from time to time when she was in school, he was a few years older that her and Sabrina.

"What's the issue?" he turned to Katie and Sabrina.

Sabrina explained the situation, yet Mack's eyes were fixed on Katie the entire time. *I already know how this is about to go,* Katie thought. Mack was in his mid-thirties and was found attractive by many, he was accustomed to having women's attention. The numerous gold Cuban link chains around his neck in addition to the gold watch on his wrist showed how flashy he was.

"I'll escort you in to handle that and we'll be done with it, cool?" Mack said amicably.

Mack saying 'handle that' let Katie know that he had not listened to a word that Sabrina said, despite him accepting the gratitude and appreciation that Sabrina offered him.

"After you," Mack said with a chivalrous yet cunning smirk, holding his hand out to allow Sabrina and Katie to walk in first.

Katie could feel Mack's eyes analyzing her from head to toe as he walked behind her. The club was loud and full of people, an environment that Katie did not miss. The smell of marijuana filled the air and bottle girls darted past quickly every few minutes. One bottle girl almost walked through Katie before Mack grabbed her by her waist and pulled her out of the way. Mack kept his arm around her waist until she forcefully moved it.

"You want a shot? I know the bouncer was coming at you wrong out there."

Mack leaned in close to her ear whenever speaking to her and would try to get closer.

"I don't drink," Katie said, scanning the crowd looking for Derek.

She hadn't made eye contact with Mack once since they had walked in.

"What? Stop lying!" Mack yelled over the music. "Come on, one shot… on me."

Katie didn't respond, still fixated on scanning the crowd. She then winced as the three of them walked past two people sloppily kissing one another on the dance floor, obviously drunk. Mack continued to look back at them as if intrigued. Sabrina tapped Katie on the shoulder and pointed towards the section where Derek and his friends were. Derek sat with his head down while everyone else stood.

"That's your boyfriend? Getting babysat?" Mack asked.

Katie ignored him again as they all began to walk in the direction of the section. As she got closer, she could see one of the women in the section recording a video on her phone to post on social media. Everyone danced and screamed into the phone as she panned around. When she got to Derek, she and a few others shared some laughs. She lifted Derek's head up to get a good shot; he was barely awake. When she put her phone down, Katie stood right in front of her with a scolding look on her face.

"Delete that," she said.

"Umm…excuse you?" the woman asked, confused.

"Don't post that. Delete it."

Sabrina felt uncomfortable as she did outside when she glanced down to see Katie's hand trembling.

"Okay girl," the woman said as she rolled her eyes.

She began to post the video on the internet right in front of Katie. Katie slapped the phone out of her hand, causing it to sail down onto the dance floor. Mack quickly stepped in between the two as they began to verbally go back and forth. Elle then appeared, staring Katie down to confront her. His eyes were low and glossy.

"Why you in here?" he asked, towering over Katie with his height.

Katie could feel the tension coming from Elle, yet she could not care less. She was never fond of Elle and had no intentions of pretending now.

"I'm taking him home. He clearly needs to go," she told him.

"We got him; he just had a little too much. We don't need you to try winning your way back right now," Elle said.

Elle's statement struck a nerve, Katie felt herself beginning to lose her composure.

"Help me get him," she turned and said to Sabrina, who was still uncomfortable and nervous.

Sabrina's eyes were fixed on Elle, who looked angry while still staring at Katie.

"Sabrina! Come on," Katie yelled.

As the two of them walked over and began to lift Derek's arms, Elle lightly began to push Katie back away from him. Katie aggressively slapped Elle's arm away. The two of them then stood face to face as if prepared to fight one another, causing Mack to step in between the two. Two bouncers saw Mack from afar and rushed over, drawing more attention to the section. Mack quickly told the bouncers to stand down.

"Look, let her get him out of here so this can be done. Go get your phone man," he told the woman whose phone was knocked out of her hand.

As she walked away, she continued shouting threats towards Katie and calling her out of her name. Katie threw Derek's arm over her shoulder and walked him out of the building, followed by Sabrina.

Derek continued to mumble; the smell of liquor hit Katie's nostrils every time he opened his mouth.

"Get in, get in, GET. IN!" Katie yelled as she helped Derek crawl into the passenger seat of her Jeep.

As she helped Derek, she noticed make up smeared on the shoulder of his black shirt.

"Alright girl, you good?" Sabrina asked.

"Yeah, thank you. You're staying here?" Katie closed the passenger door.

"I came with Sophia so I can't leave her, let me know when you make it."

Sabrina hugged Katie before heading back towards the club. As Katie drove back to her apartment, Derek was asleep in the passenger seat.

"Where we... we left?" Derek mumbled; eyes slightly opened.

Katie reached over and gently closed Derek's eyes for him to go back to sleep. After a few minutes, he suddenly began to cough and sat up, feeling around the car.

"What are you looking for?" Katie asked.

Derek suddenly tried to open the passenger door. Katie frantically grabbed him and yanked him back, causing the Jeep to swerve. Right after she pulled

Derek away from the door, she quickly grabbed the steering wheel and regained control. The swerve caused Derek to throw up on himself and on the passenger door and window.

"Oh my God," Katie said calmly and continued to drive. "You are cleaning every bit of it up too."

When they made it to Katie's apartment, it took everything in her to help him up the stairs. His shirt was covered in vomit and Katie was pressed up against it, she could not believe herself. When they made it into the apartment, she sat Derek on the couch. Derek hunched over as soon as Katie sat him on the couch, hanging his head towards the floor.

"Do you have to throw up again?" Katie asked.

Derek didn't respond but his face began to cringe. Katie quickly grabbed the garbage bin in the kitchen and put it in front of him.

"Take your shirt off."

She grabbed one of his shirt sleeves, feeling as if she was pulling on a lifeless body with how slow Derek was moving and how unresponsive he was.

"Hey," she softly slapped his face.

Derek did not respond at all.

"Hey!" She then slapped his face much harder, causing his eyes to widen for a few seconds. "Shirt. Off."

Katie was able to get the black shirt matted in vomit off Derek and tossed it in the washing machine. Derek immediately laid back on the couch and passed out. As Katie pulled a blanket out of one of the boxes in the living room, Derek's phone began to ring. She ignored it, but the person continued to call. She pulled the phone out of Derek's pocket to see three missed calls and two text messages from a Detroit phone number. Katie sat the phone on the arm of the couch and proceeded to drape the blanket in her hand over Derek. She was exhausted and just wanted to go to bed.

"I can't stand you," she grumbled as she stood over Derek for a moment.

Katie always swore to herself that she would never do things like she'd just did for anyone she dated. She felt vulnerable, which she always equated with being taken advantage of. Katie's phone then began to vibrate from receiving a text message. Her eyes widened when the same Detroit phone number came across her screen:

Hey love this is Alicia. I just wanted to hit you up, we grown. Yes me and Derek was talking in the club and he was trying to link up with me later tonight, texting me over and over. He didn't mention you. Once I found out yall were talking I knew I had to tell you. Sorry to bring it to you this late but I refused to let you be out here like a fool...I'm sorry.

Katie grabbed Derek's phone and unlocked it. When she opened it, the screen was already on the text thread between Derek and Alicia. She'd sent him several messages with no response:

Are you still coming?

Im home...

WYA??

?????

Shoulda just left with me...

Katie took a screenshot of the thread and sent it to herself. She then included the picture in her response to Alicia:

You clearly think I'm stupid. Please don't ever text my phone or his again or I will be the one talking to you woman to woman... in person.

She put both phones down and walked to her bedroom. She glanced back at Derek once more before leaving the living room.

"I really can't stand you."

CHAPTER 6

Dallas, TEXAS

Present Day | The Berry Residence

Walter woke up in a panic and glanced over at the clock to see that it was six in the morning. He quickly remembered that it was the weekend and calmed back down. Despite him abruptly waking up, Laura's face was partially buried in one of their silk pillowcases, sound asleep. Walter turned his body toward Laura and rubbed his hand along her shoulder, most of which was covered by another one of her tattoos, a large blooming flower. Walter often times couldn't help but to stare and admire her. Laura then began to mumble and talk in her sleep as she often did, causing a grin to come across Walter's face. Once she began to toss and turn, flailing her arms all over, Walter quietly rolled out of the bed surrendering the entire bed to Laura.

Waking up at six in the morning was late for him, he was usually up and moving by 5am every day. His week off was coming to an end, but he was in no rush to get back to the office. At the same time, he did not feel at peace being at home. As he sat in the kitchen drinking coffee, he thought about the trip, Laura's parents, and about Katie and Derek. He did his best to be cordial and respectful, but still felt tension between him and Katie. The dry interactions and lack thereof were obvious, nothing seemed natural. It came across to him as fake, which he also took as an insult. His phone began to vibrate across the kitchen counter, interrupting his thoughts. When he saw who it was, he let out a deep sigh before answering.

"A bit early for you isn't it?" Walter asked with his usual hint of sarcasm.

"You are really a terrible person; do you know that?" the sharp strong voice of his sister Janice came through the phone. "You seriously have a problem."

"Good morning to you too Janice," Walter said.

"You're going to the Galveston house this weekend after I asked you countless times if you were taking the trip this year, and you told me no! I had to find out from Laura that you all are going down there this weekend."

"I thought you'd be too busy on book tours and showing up on talk shows," Walter's sarcasm added fuel to the fire.

"Do not act as if I put my career over my family and stop acting like you are the only owner of that lake house! All three of our names are on that lake house. We said we would use it for family trips and getaways...I'm okay baby," Janice suddenly said away from the phone. "I'm okay I'm on the phone with JR," she let out a fake chuckle as Walter heard a door close in the background.

"I don't get the big deal, it's a last-minute decision that we made to go this weekend. You can go down to Galveston at any time. You don't need us to be there for that," he said to her.

Walter continued being disingenuous, acting as if he was oblivious to the reasons for Janice's frustrations.

"You know what I am talking about, you know why I am reacting. Don't play as stupid as you act sometimes. This little feud or hostility that you seem to have toward me is getting old, and it's childish. It's been going on for long enough," Janice said.

"Are you serious?" Walter laughed.

"Very," Janice said strongly. "I'm not the only person that sees it, it has been an obvious problem for years and I'm tired of it."

"You are overreacting over some simple miscommunication, I'm not about to go back and forth about it with you honestly. It is what it is."

Janice was someone that could get under Walter's skin like very few people could. Her demeanor, the condescending tone with which she spoke, the arrogance, and many other aspects of her character often provoked Walter. Ever since they were young, there always seemed to be competition between the two of them. Janice always had the pressing conviction to outdo Walter and be better than him, at least in Walter's eyes. Their phone call ended with Janice telling him that he needed to get bitterness out of his heart. Walter hung up in Janice's face. His ability to be rude elevated when it came to Janice. He felt even better about Janice not coming on the trip, there was more than enough for him to deal with already.

Laura walked into the kitchen a few minutes later, in her usual bathrobe. She glanced at Walter then walked to the refrigerator. Walter knew that Laura heard the conversation with Janice by the way she looked at him.

"Sounds like you had a nice conversation with Janice the other night," Walter said.

Laura continued to pull the eggs, bacon, and butter out of the fridge.

"Sounds like you did too," she said, not making eye contact with Walter.

Walter became more irritated.

"I thought we agreed that we were making this a family trip, just us?" Walter leaned on the counter towards Laura.

"Is Janice not family?" Laura asked, still not looking at Walter.

Walter frowned as Laura began to pour herself some orange juice.

"Laura, we said we—"

"No, *you* said," Laura stopped and looked up at Walter. "*We* didn't say anything. You told me that she was going to be busy this weekend and wouldn't be able to make it. I get that your brother usually flakes on us, but Janice told me that she would have rescheduled everything to come. You lied to me."

Laura slammed a carton of orange juice down and walked out of the kitchen. Walter began to walk after her but stopped himself. He learned over the years to pick and choose his battles wisely. Jared stood in one of the doorways of the kitchen, staring directly at him.

"Good morning," Walter said, reaching for his coffee mug. "You alright?"

"Are you?" Jared asked, eyebrows raised.

"Yes," Walter sipped his coffee. "Your mama just didn't get enough sleep."

"Right," Jared chuckled before he walked away.

"When did you get your hair cut like that?" Walter asked Jared, who was in the family room.

"Like four months ago."

"Oh."

Walter tried to recall when he had seen it for the first time. The comment caught him by surprise. He was able to rattle off numbers for financial analytics and reports for Anomaly in his sleep, so him being told something he didn't know was always an uncomfortable feeling. Katie then walked into the kitchen, bonnet on her head, an old t-shirt from her high school, sweats, and some house shoes. She didn't look in Walter's direction nor had she said anything to him. Walter didn't feel a pressing need to say anything to her in that moment, but felt it was the right thing to do.

"Up already?" Walter asked.

"Since five," Katie said, glancing at him with a grin on her face.

Maybe we can have a good talk, Walter thought, at ease.

"Since five? Why so early?"

"It's how I'm wired," Katie responded. "Prayed, then eventually came down here."

Walter watched as she put some fruit in the blender, preparing to make a smoothie.

"We really haven't caught up; you've been moving since you got here. How's work?"

"Umm," Katie then started the blender, causing their conversation to come to a halt.

Katie seemed as if she was trying not to look at Walter, she was so focused on the blender that it was noticeable.

"It was urgent to get that smoothie made huh?" Walter asked once the blender stopped.

Walter was a little on edge from his conversations with Janice and Laura, he took Katie's blending while he was trying to speak to her as disrespect.

"It wasn't intentional," Katie said as she poured the smoothie into a cup.

"You started the blender," Walter continued. "How wasn't it?"

"I said it wasn't intentional," she said.

"Don't worry about it, I'll let you get back to it."

"Are you serious?" Katie turned and looked at Walter. "It's not a big—"

"Don't worry about it."

Katie rolled her eyes as Walter walked out of the kitchen. Laura then reappeared, clothes changed and hair ponytailed. Walter flashed a quick grin at her, hoping to lighten up the tension but it was to no avail.

In Walter's mind, Katie was disrespectful from the moment that she and her boyfriend Derek stepped foot in his house. Starting the blender while he talked made the disrespect even more evident. As Walter walked towards the stairs, Derek appeared, still in the shorts and t-shirt that he slept in, along with a du-rag still on his head.

And then here he comes, Walter thought.

"Good morning," Derek said and nodded at Walter.

Walter simply nodded back and kept moving. He didn't have the best start to his morning. Between Janice, Laura, and Katie, he struck out regarding peaceful interactions with his family. Seeing Derek walk around his house didn't necessarily help put him at ease. Derek came off as weak to Walter, following Katie's lead and sticking to her hip, which Walter hated. He couldn't wrap his mind around how Katie could bring someone home into his house while the two of them were not on the best of terms. *How is Derek able to step foot in this house and go along with that? You're dating MY daughter. You don't know me. Yet, you come into my house and think you will disrespect me by going along with her antics?*

By noon, everyone was dressed and on the road to Galveston. Walter drove, Laura and the kids were in the car with him. Derek and Katie were in the car with Robert and Glenda. Jared had his headphones in, tuning everyone out. Tristan and Olivia both were being entertained by their digital tablets, the two of them also had headphones which completely covered their ears. Laura sat in the front seat, reading a book. The only sound in the car was the radio, which played at low volume. Walter still felt tension carry over from earlier that morning. He paid it no mind, simply focusing on the road. Laura closed her book and yawned as she turned around to look at the kids. Tristan fought to keep his eyes open, continuing to nod off as he fell asleep. Olivia glanced at Tristan before looking up at Laura, they both smiled at each other. Laura took the tablet out of Tristan's hands and took the headphones off of his ears. Tristan laid his head on Olivia's shoulder and was fast asleep. Laura's smile faded when she turned back around to look out of the passenger window, she then glanced over at Walter who was still focused on the road.

"What's important to you?" Laura asked.

Walter looked over at her, then back at the road.

"What do you mean?" Walter asked.

Laura didn't answer, she turned and looked back out of the passenger seat window. Walter felt his face begin to get hot, he did not have the patience to bite his tongue if Laura wanted to press a button.

"I mean just what I asked; what is important to you? At the end of the day, what is most meaningful to you?" Laura asked.

The question wasn't something that Walter often thought about. He just wanted to live comfortably and do it forever, and in his mind, that was the right thing to do. If he was honest, he wanted the power and control. He wanted to be in full control without depending on anyone for anything, he wanted to be at the top and he didn't feel that it was greedy or wrong to want that.

"Making sure you all don't want for anything. You all are the most important to me," Walter answered.

Laura again didn't respond. She just turned and looked back out of her window. The remainder of the drive was silent apart from the radio. Walter began to play one of his favorite nineties hip hop albums and turned up the volume a little. Sometimes drowning out the noise was the only option that he felt he had. He concluded that being the villain usually went hand in hand with being misunderstood, and he was okay with that even if it came from family.

CHAPTER 7

Katie opened her eyes wide, realizing that she'd been asleep for the last two hours. She lifted her head up from Derek's shoulder, looking out of her window to see that they were still on the highway. Glenda sat up front, looking at her cellphone as her wire-framed glasses rested slightly off her face. Robert was driving, exchanging small dialogue here and there with Glenda. Derek had one of his earbuds in, leaving the other ear open to be able to hear what was going on around him. Katie sat back and pulled out her phone to look at social media. Her feed was flooded with pictures, posts, and conversations about what happened in Charlotte the night before. Everything centered around racism, the police, and debates pertaining to if what happened was justified or excessive.

Before falling asleep, Katie talked to Miah via text about everything. Miah was numb, she didn't know how or what to feel. Her relationship with Tavares was heavily marred, she wasted most of her college years trying to change him and exhausted herself wanting better for him than he did for himself.

Her sadness was primarily for her son Deron. Despite the bad history between her and Tavares, Miah was still going to help Tavares' mother with funeral arrangements and comfort his family any way that she could. Katie didn't understand how Miah had the strength to do it.

An hour later, they were driving through Houston.

"Your old stomping grounds, baby," Glenda said to Katie.

So many different emotions hit Katie as they drove through Houston to grab something to eat. Katie hadn't been to Houston since she was in high school. She didn't have many friends from high school nor was there anyone from high school that she cared to keep in contact with.

"You'll have to bring Derek up here to see the old house when you have a chance," Robert said.

Beaches and water came into view once they made it to Galveston, which caused a sense of relaxation to come over Katie. They pulled up to a large house, not too far from the sands of the beach. The inside of the lake house was spacious despite looking smaller on the outside.

"Vacation, vacation, vacation!" Laura lifted her hands in joy as she turned around to smile at everyone.

Her phone rang and she quickly answered with excitement when she saw who it was.

"Girl, where are you?" Laura quickly walked into another room.

Derek admired the house and the view of the beach; he began to take a few pictures on his phone. Katie walked over and playfully jabbed him in the chest.

"Let's go out to the beach," she said as she hugged him.

Derek nodded, not saying anything in response.

"Pretty nice right?" Katie asked, referring to the lake house.

"It is," he said, avoiding eye contact with her.

A car suddenly pulled up quickly to the lake house which made Laura rush outside in excitement. A woman stepped out of the passenger side of the car, sunglasses covering her eyes, thick wavy hair with blonde highlights, as well as a fanny pack across her chest that covered up her red tank top shirt.

"I see you with your fine self! Alright hair! Alright hips!" Laura caused the woman to pose as if in the middle of a photo shoot.

The two of them began to go back and forth complimenting one another before embracing one another with laughs and a huge hug. Glenda ran outside shortly after, just as excited.

"You would think they haven't seen each other in years," Robert said smiling. "That's how family should be."

Katie noticed Walter quickly glance at Robert after his comment. Walter was triggered by the comment, which gave Katie a sense of satisfaction. A man got out of the driver seat to embrace Laura and Glenda also, Walter then made his way outside.

"That's Bianca's mom, dad, and her little brother Jackson," Katie said, pointing them out to Derek.

The two of them quickly changed clothes for the beach with the intention of interacting with everyone on the way out. Katie didn't desire to interact too much, she wanted to get away from everyone for a while. By the time they changed clothes, everyone was in the lake house living room, sitting and talking.

"Who is this handsome man?" Bianca's mother smiled as she looked at Derek.

"Back up auntie, this one is mine," Katie made them all laugh as she wrapped her arms around Derek.

"Ooh look at her," Bianca's mother smiled.

"This is my aunt Mel and her husband John," Katie introduced Derek.

"It's nice to meet you finally. My daughter tells me you are a really nice man and really good to my niece," Mel said to him.

Katie's eyes widened as she looked over at Derek, whose eyes also widened for a second. Derek played it off with his smile and charm. Katie was surprised to hear that Bianca spoke about Derek at all, let alone speak highly of him to her mother. Katie once again noticed that Walter seemed triggered. Though he had a smile plastered across his face, she could see right through it.

"Why didn't Bianca come? She couldn't make the trip?" Glenda asked.

"She said she has to work but then too she says she has some auditions she couldn't pass up," Mel rolled her eyes. "Don't even get me started on her."

"Right," John said.

As they all continued to talk, Derek and Katie made their way out to the beach.

"This is much needed, don't you think?" she asked as they stopped at the water.

Derek nodded, once again not saying anything in response to her. He continued to look out into the distance at the water. It was clear to Katie that Derek was disengaged.

"Okay, so what's up?" She let his hand go and crossed her arms.

"What you mean?"

"What are you thinking about? You been really quiet," she pressed him.

"I'm good, I'm just enjoying everything."

Derek didn't even try to sound convincing.

"So now that you've gotten that lie out of the way, what is up?" Katie asked again.

She remained calm despite feeling annoyed inside, it didn't take much since she was already on edge most of their time in Texas. She'd been making a conscious effort to avoid bringing that energy towards Derek.

"It's nothing," Derek looked back out at the water.

"So now there's an 'it'," Katie rolled her eyes.

"I mean… it's old, it's all good."

"Will you just…" Katie stopped herself from raising her voice.

Derek turned and looked directly at her. His stare was intense as if trying to burn a hole through her.

"Did you get pregnant by Isaac back in school?" Derek asked.

Katie felt like the wind had been knocked out of her; it was the last question that she expected to be asked.

"Where did you get that from?" Katie asked.

"It's a simple question, did you or not?" Derek looked her directly in the eyes.

For a moment, Katie was speechless.

"I thought I was pregnant for him, yes."

"So, what happened? What did you do to it?"

"It? I wasn't pregnant, I said I *thought* I was. I wasn't."

"You didn't think to tell me?" Derek asked in frustration.

"What is there to tell? I wasn't pregnant. Why would I bring up that up?"

"Just like you didn't bring up the fact that Isaac has been here and I'm not the first boyfriend who has met your family, right?"

"You found that journal…"

The blue journal was the last thing Katie wanted anyone to read; it was the one place that she was the most open and vulnerable. Much of what started as poetry quickly morphed into Katie's deepest thoughts, secrets, and feelings that she could not verbalize. She became anxious at the thought of how much Derek read and how to address it.

"I can't believe you read that, that's doing a bit much."

"You can't seriously be trying to flip this. You don't think it was a lot for me?" Derek asked. "It's things in there that we have never talked about."

"You're right," Katie said confidently. "Things I haven't talked to anyone about. Everything that's important or that impacts you, you already know. But you are naive to think that everything I've ever gone through is going to be volunteered to you. A lot of things aren't worth it."

"It's not even about something being worth it. Like… you don't trust me enough to be real with me on that level? What's the point of me even being here?"

"Why are you so insecure man? Some things are not worth arguing over or even putting out there," Katie said.

"Now I'm insecure? Man, whatever," Derek turned and began walking off.

"It's the truth! Look at you walk off. Anything that doesn't fit your ideal perception of how I should be makes you mad. You start to question everything. That's why you even read that journal to begin with."

Derek didn't respond. Katie wanted to get all her thoughts out because she didn't want to have this conversation again or even for anything to be brought up down the line.

"Do you think I'm perfect or something? I wasn't the same person in school that I am now, but I am not this flawless perception you have of me in your mind. That's just not me. But I haven't hid anything from you, there's nothing you're going to find out about me that will be malicious or hurt you."

"But you did hide something though, why do I always have to catch you up in a lie to get everything? All you need to do is be real."

"Be real about what? There is nothing for me to tell you! Do I interrogate you about all the women in the past that you smashed? Or anything you have done? No!"

"You're too secretive. For all I know, you could have had a disease or a secret kid, anything, stuff like that is—"

"What?" Katie cut him off, upset. "Now you're worried about me having a disease or some STD? You are so full of it."

Derek quickly realized how far of a reach his statement was and that he may have overstepped a boundary. The conversation struck a nerve for Katie, which is why she was so upset about it. Katie lost her virginity in college to Isaac, and she didn't do it because she was eager to do so or because she loved him. When she was cheated on in high school by Myles, she was always told that it was because she would not sleep with him. Many people used to criticize her about it, comments from Myles about his frustration didn't help. When she got to Darcy and began dating Isaac, she did not want history to repeat itself and gave up her virginity to avoid it from happening. Each time she engaged with him, it didn't feel organic or comfortable, she felt that she was doing it solely out of obligation. In the middle of their junior year, Katie began to experience serious sickness and was convinced that she was pregnant. She took a pregnancy test in her apartment which showed to be positive. Katie called her mother Laura, who had to calm her down and get her to put things into perspective, as she usually did. Katie also could not fathom the thought of her father finding out, that alone gave her serious anxiety.

When Katie went to a doctor's appointment to confirm, the doctor was able to confirm that she was not pregnant. She was relieved, and never told Isaac nor did she tell her close friends. The entire situation was the reason that she always felt the need to stand up for Miah and defend her. The two of them were in the exact same situation around the same exact time, one of them just had a completely different outcome and was crucified for it. Katie still carried a sense of guilt when hearing her friends speak negatively about Miah. Miah informed Katie that she was pregnant not knowing that Katie had just come from her own doctor's appointment.

"Look," Katie walked up to Derek and grabbed his hands. "Everything is about right now, not anything that happened before you and me. We're not eighteen; both of us are almost thirty and have been through some things. It would have been nice if we got together when we were younger and all that, but that's not our story. It's just not. You're here because you belong here, with me. That is all that matters. If other people mattered, they would be here. But for this to work, you need to be secure in right now and in the fact that you are here, not Isaac, or anybody else."

"But you didn't even tell me he's been here. You wouldn't even talk about coming here with me, but he's been here."

"Yes, he's been here, and I probably should have told you. But I didn't. I don't talk about him, I don't think about him," Katie said. "It's negative energy I don't want to bring up, I have spent years trying to forget about it."

Derek began to let his guards down, no longer frowning.

"I didn't mean to say that about the disease and the—"

"Forget it," Katie quickly said. "Just forget it, it's nothing. But is there anything else? I mean, now that you read my whole life."

Katie tried to lighten the mood with a smile. Derek looked at her and paused as if preparing to say something, then stopped himself.

"Nah," he shook his head. "I'm good."

Katie was relieved, but also surprised. There were so many other things written in the blue journal, deep things about her past relationships, her family, and especially about her father. She was not mentally prepared to address it and was relieved to not have to. As the two of them walked back, she started feeling completely different. She realized that she cared more about reconciling with Derek than she did with her father, and she wasn't sure if that was a good thing.

CHAPTER 8

The wind against Derek's face felt great as he relaxed in the passenger seat, trying to make the best of the remainder of the day. After the beach, he and Katie drove up to Houston so he could see her high school, her family's old home, and some of her favorite food places. It was evident that Katie missed their old house and missed Houston as a whole, she would light up when talking about her childhood memories. Katie didn't miss anything about high school, she talked about it as if it was the worst time of her life.

"You don't have old friends that want to see you while you in town?" Derek asked as they drove past her high school.

"No, I didn't have friends like that, not real ones anyway. The ones I'm close to don't live here anymore."

As they drove around the city, Derek couldn't help but think about all the things that he read in Katie's blue journal. Reading about Katie's feelings for Isaac and their past relationship triggered him although he didn't want to admit it. The idea that they all were in the same school at the same time and went out into the real world at the same time, yet Isaac seemed so much further along and further accomplished. Derek couldn't help that it triggered him, especially with him trying to figure life out. The feeling of being behind and trying to play catch-up was what frustrated him most. It didn't help that Katie was also successful, progressing professionally, making good money, and had quite a strong network. Derek constantly fought against the nagging thought that he was on the hot seat, fighting to keep Katie's interest and loyalty. Isaac came off as a plausible threat based on his success and accomplishments. Between how long it took for Katie to finally give Derek a chance and how he was raised to never get too attached, the perfect breeding ground for his insecurities was created.

When he read about how Katie felt about her father and read about how he treated and spoke to her, he became angry. It was a lot for him to wrap his mind around, which was why he didn't bring it up on the beach. Reading about how Walter made Katie feel and how his words and distance demoralized her is what angered Derek the most. He spoke with Troy later on the phone, explaining to him as much as he could while Katie was inside of a small store she wanted to stop by. His heart was pounding and his adrenaline was rushing as he explained to Troy what he read and how the trip was going.

"You need to stick to the game plan," Troy said firmly. "You are there to meet the family and get their blessing. You not there to address their family history."

"I'm not addressing family history; it's one person. How am I supposed to be down here connecting with him and he's tearing his family apart?" Derek paced back and forth.

"Those are her words coming out of your mouth; you don't know the whole story. That's why I say you don't need to jump into it, at least not there. Granted, she shouldn't have let you come there without filling you in, but you gotta' sit this one out."

"Then what am I supposed to do?" Derek asked anxiously.

"Play it cool. You gotta' be the standup guy coming in to see the parents. I guarantee you her dad has been sizing you up. That's why you have all that hostility from his way; he thinks you on the same wave that she is," Troy said.

It was difficult for Derek to accept Troy's advice, despite Troy always being the one to give him a proper perspective. Derek felt protective of Katie and felt like Walter needed to be confronted as opposed to everyone walking on eggshells around him. As much as Derek wanted everything to be peaceful, the urge to confront Walter was even stronger. Shortly after his call ended with Troy, Katie stepped outside of the store front, looking directly at him as he put his phone back in his pocket.

"Who were you talking to?" Katie asked, eyes fixed on Derek.

"That was Troy, asking me about some stuff at church and about the music for tomorrow."

Katie continued to give him a blank stare as she rubbed her lips together, evening out the lip gloss she'd just put on.

"The music?" she asked as she walked towards the car. "I still need to talk to Tasha about all she needs me to do."

As Katie explained to Derek what she would be doing and how she felt about it, Derek couldn't do anything but smile. Katie talked about it as if it wasn't that big of a deal, she was then taken aback when she looked over at Derek and caught him smiling.

"What are you smiling about?" Katie asked.

"I love you. You are amazing," he said to her.

Derek was not the most romantic or the best with words, so the sudden sentiment caught her off guard.

"Come on, let's get back. Been gone all day," Katie sighed. "It's been fun hanging around the city and having you here and… it was just everything."

As they drove back to Galveston, the two of them made videos of themselves singing along to songs, acting goofy and laughing. The few hours away to themselves were needed. Derek wanted to ask Katie about her and her dad, but Troy's words echoed in his mind that it wasn't the time or the place. The sun began to set by the time the two of them returned. Katie's facial expression immediately changed the moment they pulled up and saw a black Bentley truck parked in front. Derek had a gut feeling that made him uneasy the moment that he saw Katie's facial expression. Katie parked and quickly got out of the car without saying a word, something that Derek came to expect. He learned quickly that there were just things that he wasn't going to know or understand until Katie felt comfortable explaining it to him.

"What's up, ugly?"

A high-pitched voice made Derek and Katie quickly turn around. A seventeen-year-old girl ran up to them, finishing recording a video on her phone. Everything about her was festive, her dark red hair, to her numerous necklaces and bracelets, and her numerous piercings, including a septum piercing.

"Donna, what are you doing here?" Katie gave her a dry one-armed hug.

Donna was Katie's little cousin, a very annoying little cousin.

"You put some weight on, you not in shape like you used to be!" Donna yelled as she looked Katie up and down.

Katie rolled her eyes; not bothering to introduce Derek to Donna.

"Hello, beautiful. The life of the party has arrived," someone said, causing all three of them to look toward the stairs.

Katie's aunt made her way out of the house and down the stairs. She was the complete opposite of her daughter, having a sense of conservative elegance with how she dressed and carried herself. Derek's eyes widened; he immediately recognized her before she made it over to them.

"Wait...Janice Clayton is your family?"

"Relax," Katie said to him, then walked towards her aunt.

Janice Clayton was a well-known author, entrepreneur, and hosted a national talk show for several years before retiring from television and focusing on other endeavors. Despite no longer hosting a talk show, she was often on television doing interviews and making guest appearances. Derek's mother Gloria watched Janice's show often back when Derek was in middle school and high school.

Katie walked over and gave Janice a long hug. Janice's husband, Rich, then appeared not too far behind. Rich was seven years younger than Janice, and it was clear that she was the much stronger and dominant personality. When Katie introduced them to Derek, it was simple and easy without many questions and unnecessary small talk, something Derek appreciated.

"I don't know where your ugly daddy is. I was looking for him, but him and Laura aren't up there."

"They probably went somewhere," Katie said.

"Rich," Janice hissed.

She then signaled towards the truck, causing Rich to hurry and begin to unload the bags out of the truck. Janice rolled her eyes and shook her head, losing patience.

"They didn't tell me you were coming," Katie said.

"Oh, I'm sure, because they don't know," Janice said with a sinister grin on her face. "I decided to surprise them."

When Janice walked past Katie towards the house, Katie looked back at Derek with her eyes wide. Derek realized that the evening had a lot more in store than he may have been ready for.

CHAPTER 9

The breeze coming off the water made the beach all the more soothing as Walter walked alongside Laura. He and Laura were able to step away for a few hours and enjoy time to themselves. After a shaky morning, he wanted to spend some time with her to ease the tension. The time away from the kids and the in-laws proved to be all that Laura needed to relax. For a moment, Walter began to forget about work and everything else.

"You needed this," Laura said, grabbing Walter's hand.

Walter was unable to deny how good it felt for just the two of them to step away.

"I know I've probably been a little unbearable as of late," he said.

"You're human. We all have our moments."

Walter rarely said when he was wrong to anyone, but Laura was one of the only people that always was able to get through to him. He valued Laura's perspective and it wasn't solely because she was his wife. Walter valued Laura's intellect. Despite the two of them not always seeing eye to eye, Walter viewed Laura as someone of high intelligence, and he respected that about her. So, when she said things to him, he attached merit to it. On the flip side, it was also what drove him crazy when she didn't see or understand his perspective.

When they made it back, Walter's smile immediately faded at the sight of the black Bentley truck that was parked out front. The feelings of peace and relaxation that Walter had were suddenly replaced by tension. He then looked over at Laura.

"I don't know anything about it," Laura shrugged. "I did not know they were coming."

Walter quickly walked towards the lake house, being followed by Laura. The sound of music and laughs could be heard more and more as they got closer, the voice of his sister Janice was distinct. Everyone turned and looked at the two of them when they walked in. Janice immediately stood up as she and Laura yelled in excitement before they greeted one another with a long hug. The two of them were very close. Janice was always one that embraced Laura and was always there for her when she battled with serious anxiety and sickness.

As Janice and Laura talked and laughed, Walter looked around to see that everyone was playing cards, listening to music, and eating. The kids played video games that required them to dance and be interactive. Robert and Glenda watched them play while relaxing on the couch. Janice, her husband Rich, Mel and her husband John, Derek, and Katie were all at the table playing cards.

Rich stood up to greet Walter, who shook his hand and offered a lifeless greeting. Walter had no issues with Rich, but did not have much respect for him either. He hated how Rich allowed Janice to run all over him. Walter knew he couldn't have a man to man conversation with Rich because whatever they talked about always got right back to Janice. After speaking briefly with Rich, Walter was then approached by Janice. The two of them stood face to face as everyone spoke and greeted one another.

"Surprise!" Janice smiled and took a sip of her drink.

Walter hated the smirk on Janice's face.

"Come on now, we are all having fun. Keep it cute," Janice said quietly.

Walter glanced behind Janice to catch Katie watching the two of them. Katie slowly looked away, not concerned about whether Walter saw her or not.

"Good to see you," Walter said.

He and Laura then joined everyone at the table to play cards with them.

"JR knows how to play some cards now, don't sleep on him!" Janice said as she dealt the cards out.

Walter could play any card game and was very competitive. In his younger years, he made a lot of money gambling, but lost a lot of money also. Playing cards, the blackjack table, betting on horses, Walter could do it all. He began to open up more as the night continued, laughing and joking. It was rare for Walter to be seen laughing or joking. Such lightheartedness looked sort of unnatural coming from him. In the midst of everyone enjoying themselves and having fun, Walter kept glancing at Katie, who was unsure of how to respond to it. She leaned back on Derek's chest while playing cards most of the night, using him as her comfort.

"It just feels good to be away and be around family, people at work make my nerves bad," Mel said, receiving everyone's agreement.

"It's rare to get away with your family. Hard to do these days. Something always coming up," John said. "But we gotta' do it."

"Very true, and here we are," Walter smiled.

"Yep, we in here, we all in here, living the life," John said before holding up his drink.

"I just gotta' get through to this one over here," Walter nodded his head toward Katie. "I don't know how happy she is to be around me."

Walter laughed to keep everything light and easygoing.

"Stop," Katie shook her head.

"My own daughter, first born, I can't get through to her sometimes," Walter said. "I can't get through to her, John!"

Walter laughed, but John's smile seemed forced and awkward.

"Aww, Katie you been neglecting your dad?" Janice asked, finishing up dealing cards.

"No, I haven't. He knows I don't have a problem with him," Katie said.

She kept a fixed grin on her face as she began to get uncomfortable.

"Oh, you don't?" Walter asked, focused on his hand. "We haven't talked in years."

"Uh-oh," Rich said, eyebrows raised.

Rich was under the assumption that it was all just playful banter.

"Whose fault is that?" Katie asked. "When's the last time you reached out to me?"

"Oh! JR?" Janice sat back in her chair, dramatically instigating the situation.

Mel looked over at Janice; scolding her. She did not like what Janice was doing.

"Don't. You know you've had an issue with me. It's been going on for some years now. Come on, we know what's goin' on," Walter said, putting a card down on the table.

Katie tried her hardest to focus on the game and not on Walter. Walter knew that she was trying to avoid the conflict, but he also knew that if he continued to press that he would get her to engage with him. He knew his daughter well; it was like dealing with a younger version of himself. Having a few drinks opened Walter up a little, but he was far from drunk.

"Like I said…" Katie looked over at Walter for the first time. "I don't have a problem with you. It's old. The past is the past."

"So, now there's an 'it'? What's old? What's the past?" Walter pressed further.

Walter then noticed Derek staring at him with a piercing stare as if he was ready to pounce on Walter at any moment. He also glanced down at Katie's hands, noticing them begin to tremble.

"JR, stop," Laura said to him. "Just play."

Mel and the others glanced back and forth among one another, keeping their silence. Janice's eyes were fixed on Katie, looking to stir up some controversy.

"Now everybody is quiet?" Walter asked. "Come on now, we still having a good time, right?"

"Not if you don't stop killing the family vibe," Janice said.

A few of the others laughed, trying to ease the tension.

"Please," Walter said with a proud smirk. "I carry the family vibe."

Janice then looked over at him, no longer smiling.

"I'm talking about at this table," Janice said.

"That's what you say." Walter took a sip of his drink. "But it's always a loaded chamber with you, isn't it, sis?"

"I think you've had enough." Laura grabbed Walter's cup.

"No, Laura, he's not even drunk," Janice said, eyes on Walter. "This is what he does: always thinks he is being attacked. It's always him against the world."

"Is that what it is?" Walter's smile faded. "I tell the truth; people just can't handle it. The honest ones are always the villains, always. I brought up a family issue amongst family. Y'all like to keep quiet and brush things under the rug."

"And you?" Katie suddenly asked, fed up.

"Katie," Laura stepped in. "Everybody just relax—"

"Nah babe, no. She's grown, let her speak," Walter interrupted Laura. "Obviously she has some things to say, so let's get to it."

Katie stood up, not responding to Walter.

"I'm not doing this," Katie said as she began to walk away.

Derek followed her as everyone pleaded with her to sit back down.

"I'm giving you the chance to talk about it. You're not about to keep walking around under my roof disrespecting me," Walter raised his voice.

"You don't deserve my respect," Katie quickly turned and walked back towards Walter.

"Come on, chill," Derek put his arm around her, Katie quickly pushed it off.

"What did you say to me?" Walter stood up and slammed his hand of cards onto the table.

"The dad I had when I was younger was who I respected. He has been gone; I don't know who you are. Everybody can see it but you," Katie said. "You created these problems. *You* cause the family problems. *You* are the problem."

Walter could see that a switch flipped in his daughter. Katie no longer avoided the confrontation. There was a dark and intense look in her eyes. Walter never saw that level of emotion from her before, but he didn't care either.

"I'm the problem? After all I have done for this family and for you especially, I'm the problem? The balls on you to even say those words. I give up and sacrifice for everybody! I put you in position— "

"I don't care!" Katie yelled. "I don't care what you have done for everybody else! I'm talking about me!"

Glenda quickly gathered the kids and escorted them outside. She told Jared and Donna to watch them. Glenda didn't want them to hear the argument, unsure of how much it would escalate.

"The only reason you throw your money around and do the most is to compete with uncle Jeff and Aunt Janice, you always try to compete with them. You tried grooming me so I could be your little trophy to show off. Ever since I developed a mind of my own, you hated it. You saw me as competition because Walter Berry doesn't like to be showed up."

"You clearly forget all that's been done for you. Your problem is that you have always been entitled, thinking that everything revolves around how you feel, and people always catered to that. I always presented life to you straight, I didn't sugar coat things for you. People babied you your whole life and I was not one of those people. I prepared you for the real world, you should be thanking me," Walter walked towards Katie.

"Thanking you? Thanking you for what? Breaking me?" Katie said with a slight tremble in her voice, causing Laura and Mel's eyes to widen. "You used to be my everything growing up. I mean, you were such a big part of me. But you changed, you became who you are now. You became about self and your career. I never wanted to leave Houston, I was perfectly fine being close to the family and I would have been content there, I was okay. But you drove me away and made me never want to come back. You turned on me and chose your reputation and status over me, over Jared, over all of us."

Despite everyone being taken aback by what Katie said, Walter became more and more angry. He didn't care what Katie said, he was tired of being labeled as the cause of everyone else's problems. Listening to Katie's words pushed Walter to the edge of his patience.

"You do well in corporate, you fight hard to cater to everybody there. Yet you are failure in everything else. As a father, everything. You are failing as—"

"No, no, no, stop that BS right there!" Walter yelled, causing Katie to flinch.

Walter was already fuming, hearing 'failure' was gas on the fire.

"All that I have done, and you have the nerve to talk about failure? Look around you!" Walter threw his hands up. "I've been making sure this family eats! I've been putting everybody on my back! Failure? You claim I drove you away and was against you? I made sure you had a future! Was I against you when I paid off Laney in a settlement and got her and her people to drop the charges they had ready for you?"

Katie's eyes widened.

"Yeah, I know you didn't know that. Your life could have been ruined before it even started, lawsuit, assault charges, they were going for all of it. Yet you sit here and accuse me of being against you, ridiculous."

Katie's eyes began to tear up, the fixed scowl of anger still on her face.

"You still don't understand," she quietly said.

"There is nothing to understand," Walter dismissed her. "You're entitled, ungrateful, and you—"

"That's enough of that," Derek said as he stepped in front of Katie, now face to face with Walter.

Everyone was startled when they saw Derek step in front of Walter. They didn't think the atmosphere could grow any more intense, but they were wrong. Katie looked at Derek, eyes wide. Tears rolled down her face as her heart began speeding up. Walter was surprised by Derek stepping into his face, challenging him. *Who is he trying to put on a show for?* Walter thought to himself. *Who does he think he is?* Walter was fired up by Katie's words, but Derek's boldness—insolence even—gave him the outlet that he wanted to truly unleash, and that is what he intended to do.

CHAPTER 10

The entire moment was overwhelming, it was too much. Katie was drained of all of her energy and her head was throbbing. Many of the emotions and thoughts that were suppressed for years were pulled out of her, bringing her to a place of vulnerability and discomfort. Her hands still trembled from the anger that was inside of her. Everything was overwhelming for her and beginning to be too much.

"Do you know what you're doing?" Walter asked calmly. "This is family business that doesn't concern you."

Katie knew from Walter's smirk that he didn't take Derek seriously.

"*She* is my business." Derek pointed at Katie.

"Oh, she's your business?"

Walter laughed in Derek's face. His laugh then faded as he looked at Katie.

"You his business?" Walter asked her, pointing at Derek.

"I'm right here. You not talking to her, you talking to me," Derek regained Walter's attention. "All of that heavy talk is done."

"Derek, stop, don't do this," Katie grabbed his arm.

Derek calmly pushed Katie's hand off his arm.

"Nah, he been going up all night and I can't let that rock," Derek said.

"*You* can't let it? Oh, okay," Walter nodded. "You come down here, nut up and run up behind my daughter the whole time. You couldn't even approach me like a man. But now you want to flex some muscle? Who do you think you are?"

"You talking to your own daughter like she just another person on the street. What kind of man are you?"

"What kind of man am I? Let's get into being a man since you want to mention it. Let's get into it. She's your business, right?" Walter pointed at Katie. "Is that your wife? Last I checked, her last name is still Berry. This is my daughter, my seed. You are what? A boyfriend? A boyfriend, right? You come, and you go; you might be on your way out tomorrow. I don't see a ring on her finger. Matter of fact, it took the longest for you to make it to this point, to even be here. Tells me a lot about what kind of man you are. She was so hesitant to bring you here."

"That's because of you; you drove her to stay away from here. It's not about what kind of man *I* am," Derek said.

"Oh, but it is. She's smart, beautiful, has money, comes from money, and could have anybody. *Anybody*. That's why this lapse in judgement is so beyond me!" Walter began to get animated. "She goes and finds you, a nice little lap dog to do whatever she tells you, because you pacify her, you won't challenge her, step up to her. She the one leading you. The one who jumps from job to job, don't have life figured out, trying to make some ends meet. How long do you think you will last?"

Katie then noticed Derek's hand balling into a fist.

"Don't you ever disrespect me in my own house. The one I pay for you to be a guest in. Sleeping with my daughter don't make you a man," Walter said as he stepped closer to Derek. "Don't try to build yourself up and flex some muscle by trying to step to me, trying to make yourself a hero. But see, you do that because what more do you bring? What kind of man am *I*? What kind of man are you?"

Walter suddenly pushed Derek hard, sending him flying back. Rich, Robert, and John quickly ran and stood between the two of them, followed by Laura, Mel, and Glenda screaming at Walter. As much of the commotion happened, Katie felt herself going into a blackout for the first time in a long time as she tried calming Derek down. Rich, David, and John had Walter on the opposite side of the room, going back and forth with him. Glenda and Mel grabbed Laura, both trying to calm her down as she became frantic. Janice stood in the middle of it all like a deer in headlights, not attempting to stop the situation on either side. Jared and Donna suddenly ran in from outside, looking around in shock.

"What happened?" Jared asked Katie.

Katie didn't respond as she fought to keep herself in front of Derek, trying to talk to him as he continued brushing her off.

"What is the matter with you?" Laura asked Walter, seeming to be out of breath.

Everyone's eyes suddenly shifted to Laura as she began to sway back and forth, losing her balance. Walter and everyone else rushed towards her as she fell to the ground, catching her just before she hit her head. Katie quickly ran and got on the ground beside her mother, who was unconscious and unresponsive. All the air had been sucked out of the room. When Laura collapsed, it was as if nothing prior had happened. Panic spread across the room when Laura didn't appear to be breathing...

CHAPTER 11

There was always a discomfort and uneasy feeling that accompanied hospitals. From the aroma in the air, to the several doctors and nurses rushing back and forth, to the defeated look on the faces of those in the waiting room, all of it could wear a person down. The uncertainty that gripped a person the moment they walked in could be haunting. However, hearing good news proved to be a major weight lifted off of the family's shoulders after being in the hospital for quite a while. Laura, who was now fully conscious, was hooked to an IV with everyone sitting along her bedside. She was her usual self, speaking with everyone and downplaying what happened to put people's minds at ease. Walter, despite being in the midst of everyone in the room, was estranged from everyone. No one spoke to him.

Derek, Rich, and Janice were the only three that weren't in the room with the rest of the family. Janice stayed close to Rich, clamping onto this arm, speaking to him with a sense of nervousness as if afraid of how everyone would react to her. Derek sat across from them, the confrontation with Walter continued to replay over and over in his mind. He couldn't think about anything else, still angry and humiliated. Each time he thought about what happened, he became more and more upset. It wasn't just the fact that Walter pushed him, but everything that he said were words that cut deep. Derek had no desire to reconcile, he wanted to fight.

"Hey man," Rich sat next to him, putting his hand on Derek's shoulder. "You alright? I know it's been a crazy night; things just got a little out of control."

Derek didn't respond nor did he make any eye contact with Rich. Rich simply nodded and pat Derek on the back before leaving him alone. A few people did double takes looking at Janice, recognizing her from television. Katie then appeared, walking towards Derek. She looked exhausted, eyes glossy and face red. Janice and Rich stood up to embrace her.

"She's fine. The doctors don't know what happened with her but they're keeping her here overnight."

"Good, I'm so glad she's okay," Janice said.

Katie then walked over to Derek and wrapped her arms around him. Derek had one arm around her, not wanting to hug her at all.

"We probably need to get moving," Janice said as she put her jacket on.

Katie asked Rich and Janice to take them to the airport, she wanted to go home. Her grandparents Robert and Glenda understood; Laura understood also although she was not happy about it. Rich and Janice drove Katie and Derek back to the house so that they could get their things. Jared and Donna stayed behind to watch the kids, most of which were sleep. Jared was upset about all that happened and sad about his sister leaving. Katie gave him a long hug.

"Love bro, sorry about all of this," Jared said as he shook Derek's hand and hugged him.

Katie gave both Olivia and Tristan forehead kisses as they slept. She knew how upset Olivia would be when she woke up, and the thought of it ate Katie up inside. She didn't realize how much she missed her family until she was preparing to leave. The ride to Houston was completely silent. Katie found flights back to Charlotte that were scheduled to leave late at night and booked them, paying for both. When she just paid for things on impulse, Derek sometimes felt as if she was saying that she didn't think he was able to. In that moment, he had no desire to argue, mind still on all that happened.

"You haven't said anything to me all night," Katie said once they made it to their gate.

Derek didn't respond, continuing to look around the airport.

"Thanks for the flight," he finally said.

He then pulled the hood of his sweatshirt over his head. Katie rubbed her eyes then ran her hand through her hair.

"Can you please—"

"What is there to talk about?" Derek snapped. "Everything has been said."

"Why do you have an attitude with me? Like I did something to you?"

"How did he even know what he was saying? What made him even say that?" Derek looked over at Katie, anger all over his face.

"You think I had something to do with that?" Katie asked, hand on her chest.

"You been telling him my business, talking about me to him," Derek said. "That's why he talked all that BS. You probably feel just like he said, I'm just some last resort after your last relationship failed. Then you waited this late to bring me here, yet ole boy been up here and spent time with your family. I look like a fool."

"You cannot be serious right now. I don't have a great relationship with him as you can see," Katie leaned in close to him. "I should have told you about my situation with my dad, I own that."

93

"Seems like you got a lot to own," Derek said. "You let me come out here and get blindsided, I came into a situation that was already hot."

"I said I own that, but I'm not talking down on you to anyone...and none of what he said is true. I don't feel like that about you. You know that," Katie pleaded.

"Just stop talking to me about it. You had me thinking I was the first one you were ever bringing home, now I'm supposed to believe what you're telling me now right?"

Katie didn't respond, she had no words.

"Right?" Derek repeated himself.

He then put his headphones over his ears and leaned back against the window with his hood over his face. Katie sat in the same position for a few seconds before she sat back in her chair and turned away from Derek. Despite her frown, she couldn't stop the tears from rolling down her face. The two of them didn't speak for the rest of the night, not even on their flight home to Charlotte. There was no dialogue between the two. When they landed in Charlotte, there was no hug or kiss between the two and nothing was said. Derek didn't feel the need to try nor did he want to, the two of them went their separate ways and honestly, Derek wasn't sure if it was for good...

CHAPTER 12

Charlotte, NORTH CAROLINA

Troy Loren was losing his mind, scrambling back and forth to clean up his kitchen and calm a raging two-year-old. Food was plastered, spilled, and scattered all over the floor and the walls. His son Chad ran around naked, screaming and laughing undoing the cleaning faster than Troy's hands could work. When Troy's phone began to ring, he rushed to it in desperation, relieved.

"Joy, are y'all almost here like...what's up?" Troy asked his sister.

"Oh my God, yes. We're pulling up," Joy said, annoyed before hanging up the phone.

Derek sat on the couch, trying to hold in his laughter as he watched Troy. Chad then ran full speed towards Derek, huge smile on his face and food smeared across his mouth. As Derek braced himself for Chad, Troy suddenly stepped in front of Derek and picked Chad up in mid-run.

"You have run your last lap, sir!" Troy yelled to Chad; whose face puffed into a pout. "Nah, ain' no crying bruh."

Derek then broke down laughing as Troy's younger sister Joy walked in through the front door, followed by Troy's wife Shanice. Shanice looked as if she was going to pop out their second baby at any moment. Chad immediately began to reach for her.

"Ooh you are dirty chile'," Shanice grabbed him as he clamped tightly to her. "Did you have fun with daddy?"

"No!" Chad yelled, frowning at Troy, causing Shanice to chuckle as they walked upstairs.

"Whew, they had fun alright," Joy said, eyes wide as she walked towards the kitchen.

"I don't want to hear it," Troy said, trying his best to clean up. "Now is not the time."

"You left him hanging?" Joy asked Derek jokingly.

"It was already a wrap when I came in!" Derek held his hands up in innocence.

Joy was only a year younger than Derek. She was one of the lead singers on the praise team at church, so they saw each other often for rehearsals.

"How was that date?" Troy asked.

"Let me tell you… I walked out as soon as I walked in," Joy said. "Dudes be so fine until they open their mouth. He pulled out my chair for me, looked good, smelled good, everything. Then he said, 'wow, you are so beautiful for a dark-skinned woman'."

Joy's comment made Derek and Troy's mouths drop.

"I said, 'what does that mean?' I was trying to give him the chance to you know, clean it up. He goes, 'no it's a compliment, you know it's rare that someone is highly attractive like you are with your complexion'."

"Idiot," Troy shook his head.

"So, I got up and left. I already told Shanice I was going to do her hair anyway, so I just texted her and met her at the store. I just don't have time for the ignorance. I didn't expect anything of substance to come out of his mouth after that," Joy said. "It's hard out here. Be glad y'all found y'all people."

"Amen to that," Troy said as he and Derek glanced at one another.

Once Shanice came back downstairs, Troy and Derek went outside to talk. Derek spoke with Troy over the phone earlier in the day after Troy got out of church and explained to him everything that happened while in Texas. Derek didn't attend church because he was exhausted after having not slept. Troy informed him that Katie didn't show up to church that morning either. After brunch and quality time with his family, Troy told Derek to come by to talk. Derek was anxious to talk to someone about what happened, there was so much going on in his mind and he needed to get it out.

"So…what now?" Troy asked, leaning against his car in the driveway.

"I'm just about to let it all blow over, figure out what's next."

Derek looked completely lost as he sat on the hood of his car, a complete one-eighty from the last time Troy saw him.

"How is Katie feeling?" Troy asked.

Derek shrugged carelessly.

"You haven't talked to her?"

"She good, I don't need to check on her," Derek said pridefully.

"What about the proposal then?" Troy asked.

"Man," Derek let out a loud sigh and looked off into the distance. "I'm just trying to process this whole weekend right now so…I don't know."

"Don't know when or know if you will do it?" Troy asked.

Derek looked at Troy but didn't respond, the look on his face said it all.

"Why you mad at her? You got into it with her dad and all that, so why is there a problem with her?"

"She set me up for that!" Derek hopped off the hood of the car. "She led me into that whole situation. I had to learn how much she lied about when all of it blew up in my face, had me looking stupid."

"But you stepped in it, right?" Troy asked.

"To defend her," Derek said, leaning back against the car. "He was going stupid on her, I can't just sit and let that go on. What would I have looked like?"

Derek's tone made it evident that Troy's questions began to frustrate him.

"It sounds good, but that's not the reason you jumped in it. You mad and it has nothing to do with Katie, you not even mad that her pops came at you. I told you on the phone to stick to the game plan. You went in and tried sticking your chest out, trying to show yourself. That's why you jumped into the situation," Troy said. "You tried showing out, trying to show yourself to be something."

"What are you talking about?" Derek raised his voice. "What do I have to prove to anybody?"

"You tell me!" Troy yelled.

"Come on man," Derek shook his head. "You sound ridiculous."

"Some insecurities got triggered. You got humbled and it's killing you because you have been questioning yourself already. You had doubts about yourself before you left, and still not thinking straight right now."

"Help me understand it then bro, since you got the answers," Derek said sarcastically.

"Be real with yourself. You stepped to that man trying to prove something to yourself and wasn't ready for the smoke. You mad because you are triggered. Katie got it first, then her mama had to go to the hospital, and you can't even think about that because you got pressed."

None of what Derek was told was anything that he wanted to hear. He just felt as if no one sympathized with what he went through.

"Wow man…" Derek shook his head. "You really made this all about me, everybody else was cool. I'm the one trippin' right?"

Troy didn't respond.

"I got work tomorrow," Derek said, getting into his car.

"You just leaving bruh?" Troy held his hands out in disbelief.

"Y'all not getting it," Derek said in anger. "I'm just tired of talking about it at this point. I'll get at you later gang."

Before Derek could pull off, Troy walked over and knocked on the driver side window.

"You my brother, I'll never not tell you what's real. I'm not saying her dad wasn't wrong. I'm saying your anger is misplaced; you're not seeing the situation clearly. You not mad at the right thing, and you about to ruin what you have over it."

As Derek pulled off, Troy walked back into the house. Derek hadn't felt as flustered as he was in a while. It was a feeling that he hated, and he remembered how it felt the last time...

CHAPTER 13

Charlotte, NORTH CAROLINA

Two Years Ago.

The brightness of the sun and clear blue sky heralded a new day, much different from the gloomy dark night of a few hours prior. Derek could barely see anything the moment he opened his eyes, the sun shined directly on the couch where he was. The moment he turned his head, he immediately winced as shooting pains went all throughout his head. The headache amplified even more when he sat up and scrambled for his phone. When he saw the time and several missed several calls, he jumped up in a panic. Church service was set to begin in half an hour, and he was supposed to have been there an hour beforehand. As soon as he jumped up, Katie walked out of her bedroom. She wore a long t-shirt that went down to her knees, and most of her hair was pressed down while a small remaining section stuck out, waiting to be pressed down.

"We gotta' go!" Derek yelled. "I was supposed to be at the church at nine!"

Katie didn't know what to say as she watched as Derek continue to scramble in a panic. She pointed him in the direction of the shower in the other bedroom, which would belong to Bianca once she moved in. Katie already ironed Derek's clothes for him. She had been up since six in the morning despite going to bed at three in the morning. Derek brought clothes with the intention of spending the night, which changed after their argument the day before. Katie looked up the church online while Derek was asleep to see the service time, but she was unsure if they still planned to attend. Derek took a quick shower and got dressed, then began to rush Katie. When they walked up to Katie's Jeep, Derek paused for a moment as he stared at the vomit that was all over the passenger side window.

"Come on, get in," Katie said calmly, not acknowledging the vomit.

Derek couldn't help but to frown at the smell in the Jeep as Katie sped through the streets of Charlotte, unbothered behind her sunglasses. Although he hated how reckless Katie drove, he didn't complain since they were late. All Derek could think about was how he would explain himself and the worst-case scenarios of him not being at church on time. His mind continued to race, and he was angry that he allowed himself to be in the position that he was in. When they pulled up to the church, Derek quickly got out of the Jeep and ran towards the front doors, leaving Katie behind.

"Thanks for waiting on me," Katie sighed.

Part of her contemplated not going inside and just driving home, she felt even more stupid about going to get Derek the night before. She got out of her Jeep and took her time walking up to the front doors, her heels prevented her from running or walking fast. By the time she made it in, her slight irritation grew into a full-blown attitude that she didn't care to hide.

"Hi! Welcome! We are glad to see you!" one of the greeters enthusiastically walked up to her and handed her a program.

Katie forced a smile, trying not to be rude. She began looking around, trying to figure out where to go as there were several people walking in many different directions. As she looked around, she caught the stare of a woman standing across from her. *What is she looking at, all in my face? Church folks know they can be weird.* To Katie's surprise, the woman then began to walk directly over to her as if she read Katie's thoughts. The woman wasn't smiling at all.

"Hi," Katie said, putting on a smile. "Can you tell me—"

"You can just stop," the woman said, beginning to grin.

"What?"

"I know a fed-up face when I see it. You don't have to put on for me."

Katie didn't contest and let her guards down, no longer smiling. The woman signaled for Katie to walk with her.

"That bad?" Katie asked.

"If 'I'm ready for whatever' was a face," the woman said, making Katie laugh.

"I'm not trying to be like that, it's just been a rough morning."

"I understand. Come on, sit with me today, I'm Tasha by the way."

Katie was making her way into the sanctuary while Derek was rushing down the hallway which led to the administrative offices. The lobby became a hallway that circled all the way around the sanctuary the further one walked down. The administrative offices were behind the sanctuary and pulpit. He could hear the music, which gave him a sense of relief that service wasn't hindered because he wasn't up there. Before he could make it to the back, one of the elders of the church came out of one of the back rooms, eyes locked in on Derek as if he'd been expecting him. The elder towered over Derek, a tall man, head full of grey hair, in a grey three-piece suit.

"Elder Daniels—"

"Let me talk to you," he cut Derek off and escorted him in the back hallway.

Derek walked past one of the mirrors in the hallway and caught a glimpse of himself. He had deep bags under his eyes, clothes were loose and somewhat hanging off of him, and his eyes were red and glossy.

"Might wanna' get the rest of that stamp off of your hand," Elder Daniels said to him.

Derek looked at his hand to see a stamp from the club was still there.

"What is going on?" the Elder asked.

"I overslept man, I'm sorry. I really—"

"We trusted you to be here and you didn't even show."

"I know, I—"

"If Wendell didn't miss his flight, nobody would be out there on the keyboard!"

Derek didn't respond. All he could do was take the admonishment.

"I know you didn't oversleep; I smell the liquor on your breath. The mouthwash ain' covering it."

Derek looked up at him like a deer caught in headlights.

"I'm a former alcoholic, been sober for eight years. Trust me, I know," Elder Daniels said. "Keep it real with me."

Derek was hesitant to speak his mind; he didn't know what to say that would be a good enough excuse. The longer he stood in front of Elder Daniels, the more he realized he didn't have a valid excuse.

"I was going through a lot. I just needed to take my mind off things," Derek said.

"And that means go get drunk and negate your responsibilities? You start going through something, and you just ran to some liquor and the club, and now you get here late and got a whole new set of problems. You're a man, face things like one. Men don't run."

The two of them, despite speaking louder than Derek would have liked, couldn't be heard due to the singing and the music echoing through the hallway.

"You need to decide what road you're going to take, today. If you are going to follow God and start doing things His way, you can't address your problems like you used to. You can't be a man that just goes to church on Sunday and live completely different during the week, especially if you plan on being one of our musicians here."

Derek became even more upset; correction was a hard pill to swallow. In his mind, there were people doing much worse than he'd done. *Why can't I at least get credit for all that I am doing right? At least I still showed up; at least I'm trying to do something. It's one mistake.* He then found himself picking Elder Daniels apart in his mind, trying to find reasons not to listen to him.

"Go and sit in the congregation, and I want you to think about what kind of man you want to be and ask yourself, how committed are you?"

"Come on Elder man, I can at least—"

"No, no, no, go sit in the congregation, and think on that," Elder Daniels insisted.

Although the music was going forth and everyone was occupied with singing, clapping, and dancing, Derek felt as if all eyes were on him. Everyone on the praise team and the musicians on stage knew that he was supposed to be up there with them. The thought of them watching him sit in the crowd ate Derek up, he kept wondering what was going through their minds and what he looked like in their eyes. He saw where Katie sat and quickly walked over and stood beside her. She sat close to the front which made Derek even more uncomfortable. Everything from Saturday replayed over and over in his mind. Looking back on it, he didn't understand how he allowed himself to get to the point of drinking and smoking. Derek sat down and buried his face in the palms of his hands. Between being exhausted, having a massive headache, and the feeling of embarrassment, he felt miserable and angry with himself. Katie then sat down and put her arm around Derek's shoulders, annoying her own self. She hated that she wanted to comfort him or that she cared to do so. She wanted to be more upset than she was. Derek wanted to direct his frustration at Katie. After being checked by Elder Daniels, he couldn't see how it made sense to direct his frustration at her. He wanted to blame everybody, and the fact that he was only able to blame himself was something that he struggled to accept.

CHAPTER 14

Present Day.

Charlotte, NORTH CAROLINA

Workdays didn't seem as unbearable as they usually did to Derek. He wanted to keep his mind occupied and not be left to his thoughts, even working after hours on some days. His boss Chuck didn't have any complaints about it, nor did he bother Derek about his work or performance. Everyone could tell that Derek was focused and did not want to be bothered. Derek hadn't spoken to Katie since they returned from Texas. He had no intention of reaching out and felt justified in not doing so. Derek also hadn't spoken to Troy since the two of them had their heated discussion in Troy's driveway. He was relieved that Bible study that week was cancelled so he wouldn't have to run into either of them.

After work, he met Elle at the gym to work out and play basketball. Derek told him all that had happened. Elle was more easygoing than most when he was in a good headspace, which wasn't always the case. There once was a time where Elle would fly off the handle, shooting first and asking questions later. As years went on, he became one of the most sensible.

"At least you didn't back down. You stepped to him like a man. Real ones know you can't do anything but respect that bro," Elle told him.

Derek could live with that. After explaining to Elle how others saw the situation, it was a relief for someone not to completely trample on his point of view.

"You know we can't win for losing," Elle said as he finished his set of bench press reps. "We either don't respect women, are insecure, or whatever else they come up with."

"Right, I thought me standing up for my girl was me doing right."

"Not just for her, for yourself," Elle pointed out. "What would they have said if you stood there and didn't say anything?"

"That's what I'm saying!" Derek yelled in relief.

"Yeah, you couldn't really win that honestly. It will blow over though."

"Nah man, I don't know. I'm not trying to be dealing with all that."

"Deal with all what?" Elle asked. "You not dealing with a lot."

Derek instantly became irritated at Elle's comment. He wanted people to be on his side and support him being upset. He wasn't looking for optimism.

"Bro, you know you not like us, right?" Elle asked.

"What you mean by that?" Derek asked.

"I should say, you not living like us now. You in a different lane now bro."

"How so? What are y'all?"

"Savages," Elle said to him. "That's not you. You switched to a different way of doing life. I'm not saying we all haven't matured or grew up, but you move how you supposed to."

"I'm no better than anybody else," Derek said as he began his set of bench press.

"Not saying you better than anybody, but you already know you not living the same way we are. You move honorable: God-fearing, one girl, trying to settle down, you not on the BS. Don't switch up. All that stuff we used to do, you past that, and that's not a bad thing."

"I get what you mean E," Derek finished his set and stood up. "But it's not even about trying to be a savage. I'm just over it. Don't feel like dealing with it. It's too much of a headache."

"Too much of a headache?" Elle frowned. "Nah, you just mad. Her pops tried you, pulled your card. Any man that get tried gon' feel like that. If she a real one to you, you need to figure that out."

"What happened to calling women out on their BS and not falling for the games though?"

"This not that. This is just this one situation. All that you read about her and ole' boy from college, charge it to the game. You remember how we all moved around that time. We call out certain types of females. Katie not one of those, at least from all I've seen. We had our issues, but she not. You your own man though, you do you. I'm just saying be real with yourself, don't try being somebody else's definition of real."

Elle left the gym shortly after when he received a call, leaving almost instantly. It wasn't uncommon for him to suddenly disappear or have something to do. Derek sat in the sauna thinking about what Elle said and about everything overall. *Don't try being somebody else's definition of real...*Those words echoed in Derek's mind, and they somehow reverberated what Troy said to him. He began to rethink the whole situation that he was in. As he sat scrolling through social media, he came across a picture that Katie posted from the airport. The picture was followed by a video of her and another woman at a restaurant.

"Look who is here!" Katie said into the camera with a huge smile on her face.

The video then switched to show one of Katie's close friends, Imani, sitting across the table doing a silly dance because she was on video. Derek remembered that Katie's close friends were coming into town for the upcoming weekend.

"Waiting on my two other baddies to get here! Where y'all at?" Katie said, turning the video back to her.

Derek closed out of the application on his phone. He couldn't deny the effect that seeing Katie's face had on him. It always felt as if he was seeing her face for the first time. Thoughts and memories from different times in their relationship began to flood his mind, good memories that he sat and meditated on. He suddenly began to grit his teeth as the words of Walter disrupted his happy thoughts. He struggled to get past it, not just the disrespect, but also the embarrassment.

"Chicago?" a voice interrupted Derek's thought.

Derek looked to see an elderly white man across from him in the sauna, wearing shorts and flip flops with a towel over his head. He was referring to the 'Chicago Basketball' t-shirt that Derek wore.

"Born and raised," Derek said to him.

The man simply nodded. "Is it as bad as they say it is?" he then asked.

Derek chuckled, shaking his head. It was a question that always got a response from him because he hated the rep that people gave Chicago.

"It's as bad as you let TV make you think it is."

"Yeah, the news shows a lot of the violence and shootings there," the man said.

"Of course, it's the news," Derek said. "That's not the whole city though."

"Facts," another man who sat in the sauna pulled his earphones off to chime in. "They won't talk about kids getting scholarships or the highest ACT scores, but you know what that's about."

"What is that about?" the elderly white man turned around the one that joined the conversation.

"Come on now, you already know what that's about! Maybe you don't," he raised his voice.

Two more men came into the sauna as they all began to have a heated discussion about racism and how blacks and whites interacted with one another. Derek left the sauna as they all began to argue. When he walked towards the front doors to leave the gym, the huge TV at the front of the gym had a breaking news story from the sports world. A woman appeared on the screen to break the story.

"In breaking news, Philadelphia has released All-Pro receiver Myles Gray this evening, making him immediately eligible to sign with another team. Gray is expected to meet with New York, Kansas City, and Dallas in the coming weeks. This release takes place weeks after private messages and audio sent on social media circulated regarding an alleged affair Gray was having with the wife of Philadelphia offensive coordinator Daniel Price. Also, some messages emerged believed to be between he and another mysterious woman. Gray is accused of threatening to ruin her life if she came forward stating that she was expecting a child with him. There also have been several other messages and information that the organization will not make public but has elected to address behind closed doors. We are told the information is quite disturbing and quote, tear the organization apart at the seams. Gray led the league in receiving yards and touchdowns two years in a row. After a heated exchange at the team's practice facility where the two had to be separated due to a physical altercation, Philadelphia GM Gene Winston had this to say about the situation…"

As she continued to report, highlights of Myles Gray came across the screen, followed by cameras and reporters following him as he and a woman whose hand he held were walking out of the Philadelphia facility towards a long black truck. Derek had a strong feeling that the woman was Laney, whom Katie's father mentioned settling out of court with. Seeing and hearing about Myles Gray now took on a whole different perspective for Derek now that he knew all that he knew. Derek instinctively was about to text Katie about what he was seeing to crack a joke but refrained from doing so.

"The irony," he shook his head and walked out of the gym.

CHAPTER 15

BERRY RESIDENCE
McKinney, TEXAS

T he evening was usually the loudest time in the house when Walter came home, but lately it was quietest. Although Walter was in a full house, he felt distant from everyone. He sat in the family room, still in his work clothes with the remote in one hand and a glass of wine in the other. The only light in the room came from the TV. His blazer rested on the back of the couch and his necktie was loosened hanging around his neck. He sat and watched an old home video. Walter and Laura had many home videos which they had converted to DVD so that they would last. Walter was watching Katie's tenth birthday party, which was recorded by Laura's sister Mel. She often came to Houston to spend time with Laura, enabling Bianca and Katie to spend time together in addition to the summers they spent together. Laura sat at the table, helping Katie cut her birthday cake. Everyone had just finished singing happy birthday and Katie had just blown out her ten birthday candles. The sound of yelling and whining then was heard, the camera turned quickly to reveal two little girls going back and forth arguing over a bike and whose turn it was to ride.

"Bianca," Mel said strongly from behind the camera. "No ma'am, no."

Bianca, who was one of the girls, let the doll go and began to pout. Laura looked up from cutting the cake and suddenly began to smile. She then tapped Katie on the shoulder, who was focused on the cake.

"Look baby, look!" Laura pointed with a huge smile on her face.

Katie looked up and immediately screamed, causing the rest of the kids to turn around and react in awe. A young Walter brought in a large pink toy Jeep that Katie wanted for quite some time. It was large enough for a child to get inside and drive it as if it was a real Jeep. Katie ran and jumped into Walter's arms, giving him a tight hug and didn't let him go. Walter couldn't help but to smile as he watched, it was bittersweet for him to watch.

"They grow up fast, don't they?" Robert suddenly appeared, standing behind the couch.

Robert and Glenda came back to Dallas with the family, helping around the house. The two of them elected to stay a little longer after Laura's incident to ensure that she got enough rest.

"They really do," Walter said, still staring at the TV. "All of it seems like yesterday."

"That's how it goes," Robert said. He then pulled off his hat and sat on the couch opposite of Walter. "So how are you holding up? You've been out of it since this past weekend. Laura has been worried about you."

Walter slowly shook his head, trying to gather his thoughts.

"Just been thinking about a lot of things. When we had to take Laura to the hospital, that was the first time I've been shaken in a long time. I thought going back to work this week would take my mind off it all but…I was reminded that it's not too bright there either."

"No?" Robert asked.

"I went back, it was as if I was just another face. Nobody cared to talk about my vacation, why I left. I could have been gone for another week and they wouldn't have noticed. I walked in, they let me know the progress we made and only wanted to talk about the numbers."

Walter looked distraught and defeated as he took a sip of his wine.

"You expected hugs, kisses, and people to miss you?" Robert asked him.

"It's just…no matter how hard I've worked or how much I do, I can't win."

"Are you crazy?" Robert shook his head. "Have you stopped and looked around here? You keep trying to win in the wrong place. Something can happen to you tomorrow; they'll send out an email with their condolences, send some thoughts and prayers, then have your replacement by the end of the day. Nothing personal, it's business. You keep trying to make it personal."

"But what's wrong with enjoying what I do? And wanting to be rewarded for it?"

"Nothing is wrong with it, but what's wrong with enjoying what and who you have here? They're the prize." Robert then sat up, staring at Walter. "You think you doing them a favor working extra? You want your job and your company to give you that love and adoration you can get right here every single day, from your family."

"I do what I do for my family," Walter said firmly.

"What more do you need to do? You got the house, cars, money, what more do you need to chase? I never worked in corporate America, but the game is the same whatever you do. When the money is always the end game, you will never stop chasing it. No matter how much you get, it will never be enough."

Walter looked over at Robert for the first time, sensing the seriousness in his voice.

"I used to play in a band, in clubs, me and all of my guys, you know this. We traveled, had women, all of that. But outside of the music, we did what we had to do. I grew up with them and we didn't have anything; came straight from nothing."

Robert had Walter's full attention.

"We ran the Midwest, but wanted more, wanted to expand. There wasn't much to come up on after a while. So, we went south, started moving around Oklahoma, Arkansas, Mississippi, all that. I met my wife when we went to New Orleans, and I ended up going back and staying there for her. I had two daughters already when I met Glenda, by two different women. They didn't want to get abortions, so I paid them to at least leave me alone. I really didn't want to deal with the two women that I had them by. If I could have just erased them out of the equation and took my two daughters, I could have lived with that but that wasn't happening, so it was what it was."

"You?" Walter asked in shock.

"Listen. So, me and Glenda got married, had Laura and Mel, and even though I felt like I wasn't ready to be somebody's daddy, I wanted to do right by those two. Glenda also was an amazing woman so

I knew I had to shape up. She also told me before the girls came that I better leave the streets alone, it was either them or the life I was living. So, I left it to my guys, bowed out, got a job. It was a small gig; music gigs were a little slow, but I still came out decent. I wasn't used to slow money. I hated working a regular job, but I did it, even got promoted. One thing about it, the addiction for them is the drugs, for you it's how fast the money comes in. It's irresistible. Then the girls were about to be in high school, I wanted to get them cars, and as much as Glenda had been good to me, I wanted to change her life. We were making it, but I wanted to get more. So, I eased my way back out there for a little bit, started my old ways. We had a situation go far left, my boys linked up with some guys from Shreveport before I got back out there. We got into a serious bind, real serious. They killed two of my buddies within one week and were looking for me. They threatened to kill me and my entire family."

Walter was blown away. Laura never told him any of this about her life, she just always mentioned that they moved away. She never went into the details of why. It was also difficult for him to picture a man as honorable as Robert being in such a situation.

"I went home, admitted to Glenda what happened, and had to uproot my family out of New Orleans. That is how we ended up in Muskogee, Oklahoma. My daughters hated me, and Glenda struggled for a long time to trust me. I mean…" Robert shook his head, reliving the emotions of that time in his life. "Laura and Mel had a lot of friends they left behind. They had to leave their lives behind, lives they loved. I moved them from family members, and everything they had going on. Not just that, but we got to Muskogee and had a very hard time adjusting and getting to some stable ground. Once Mel got old enough, she moved right back as you can see. Laura went off to school and…you know the rest with her."

There was a pause between the two of them as Walter sat there, processing everything that Robert said to him.

"I can't believe it," Walter said.

"I don't talk about it. Laura and Mel don't even know all the details of what happened with me during that time. But I told you all of that to say, I thought I was doing something the right way for my family and instead, I put them in a terrible situation. I almost lost my relationship with my two youngest daughters. That's what I'm telling you, you got a good situation and you are comfortable. I don't have a relationship with my two oldest, and barely maintained the one with my youngest two. It kills me that my oldest two want nothing to do with me. Tristan and Olivia are young, you still have them. But your oldest two, Katie and Jared, you can lose them quick. Don't lose them thinking that you are doing for them or have done for them."

"You may be right," Walter conceded.

He and Robert both turned and looked at the TV. On the screen, Walter was on one knee as Katie's small arms were wrapped around his neck, a huge smile on her face.

"After this weekend, I don't know if I'll ever get that back again, especially after I let her boyfriend have it."

The two of them laughed at Walter's statement.

"Yeah, you lost your mind," Robert said as they continued to chuckle. "You remember when we first met? I thought you were soft and couldn't protect Laura."

"Trust me, I remember it clear as day," Walter nodded with a smirk on his face.

"But," Robert said with a shrug, "now I'm talking to you about my grandkids. Things work out in time."

Robert pat Walter on the back and headed back towards one of the guest rooms.

Walter sat and reflected on everything, for the first time reflecting on himself as opposed to what others were doing. He hated the position that he was in at his job, but even more so, he hated the position that he was in with his family, a position that he realized he'd been in for a while. His phone suddenly buzzed, he looked to see a text message was from Isaac Duke: *What's up old man, I'll be in town this weekend. Still got time for a drink?* Walter stared at the text message for a moment, causing him to reflect even more.

"Do better Walter."

CHAPTER 16

Charlotte, NORTH CAROLINA

Two Years Ago

As Pastor Loren gave the benediction, people began to make their way out of the building although advised to wait until the end. Katie grabbed her purse and began to walk out, ignoring their request to wait until dismissed. She didn't wait up for Derek either. Since he left her behind on the way into church, she eagerly returned the favor. She also left quickly because she was upset by the message that Pastor Loren preached; he said quite a few things that she honestly wasn't trying to hear. Derek followed not too far behind Katie, not sticking around to fellowship as he usually did.

The ride back to Katie's apartment was silent, no music nor conversation between the two of them. Derek received text messages from his friends checking on him and sharing pictures from the night. The conversation showed Derek that they had a great time the night before, a night he could only remember in bits and pieces. Their silence continued once they made it back to the apartment. When they walked in, Katie quickly walked over to the kitchen and Derek went and sat on the couch, trying to figure out his next move.

Katie poured herself some water, kicked off her heels, and pulled one of the kitchen barstools towards the couch. She sat across from Derek and stared him down. Derek felt as if Katie's stare was burning a hole into the top of his head, making him look up at her.

"You were ready to throw it all away last night?" Katie asked calmly.

"What are you talking about?"

"Last night at the club," she said to him. "Were you ready to throw it all away?"

"What are you talking about? I'm really asking; I don't even know how I got here last night," Derek said.

He also kept his tone calm. His thoughts began to race as Katie nodded her head and walked over to the kitchen island. She didn't say anything, reaching into her purse for her phone. *What is she about to show me?* The night before was a blur to him, there wasn't much that he could remember no matter how much he tried. Katie walked back over and handed her phone to Derek, showing the picture of the text thread that she sent to herself the night before. She then sat back down in front of him awaiting a response. Derek sat, not sure what to say as he continued to stare at the phone.

"I don't remember any of this."

"Yeah, because you passed out. But before that, something made her think that you were going to her place. Y'all clearly had plans," Katie said.

Derek took a deep breath, running his hand over his face.

"I was drunk. I was high too," he confessed. "I don't remember what happened."

"I don't care," Katie said, continuing to keep her voice calm. "You went and entertained this girl, and had you not passed out, there's no telling what you would have done."

Derek sat back on the couch, still dumbfounded.

"I just told you I don't remember anything. She just happened to be there. A lot of people were there."

Katie picked her phone up off the table and pulled up the video that Sabrina sent her and sat the phone back down in front of Derek. Derek looked at the video to see Alicia, the woman Katie was referring to, sitting on his lap, touching his hair, laying her forehead against his.

"How drunk and high were you right there?" Katie asked.

Derek didn't know what to say nor did he have an immediate response.

"We have an argument and your way of dealing with it is going out and doing this?" Katie's voice began to elevate. "This is how you handle things?"

"Doing what? Nothing happened. Should she have been on me? No, I'll give you that. But it's not like I slept with the girl," Derek's voice also elevated.

"How do I know that? You were out with Preston, who we all know gets around, then Elliot who pushed me last night by the way. Yet I'm supposed to assume they gave you some good advice and wasn't trying to put you on hoes? Please."

"So, you mad at me because of a girl I have no ties to, and I didn't do anything with. But we can't talk about you spending time with your ex. How does that work?"

Katie sighed, rubbing her eyes in frustration.

"I'm not about to keep having this same conversation with you. It was lunch. I wasn't in a club, I wasn't sitting on his lap, I—"

"How is that okay!?" Derek suddenly yelled.

"Because I wasn't with you!" Katie screamed back at him.

Derek sat back on the couch and laid his head back. There was a moment of silence as the two of them sat and faced each other. Derek knew that he shouldn't have put himself in the predicament he was in. The whole morning was a disaster. He felt that he'd lost in every situation and knew there was no point in fighting any more battles. Any lead way he felt that he had was thrown out of the window with the video of Alicia sitting on his lap and in his face. It didn't help that Alicia was someone that Katie was not fond of.

"And in case you didn't know, she was ready to pin it all on you," Katie said as she showed Derek the message that was sent to her. "You thought you had a friend? Y'all will learn one day: women are calculated and can be devious; men are sloppy… and dumb."

Derek didn't respond. Katie then grabbed his phone as well as her own.

"Look, I'm willing to forgive and forget," Katie continued.

She held Derek's phone up and deleted the text message thread between him and Alicia. She then tossed her phone over to Derek. Her phone was open to the thread with the pictures of her and Isaac, the thread that caused everything. Derek looked at Katie's phone, then looked up at her.

"If you can't let it go or feel like you can't forgive me for hurting you, don't delete it. But if you can forgive and are willing to move on like I'm willing to, then do it. If you were anyone else, I wouldn't care. I would have left you to yourself last night and just let it be what it was. But I know how long it took for us to get to this point, and I don't think I'm crazy when I say we both could see this being something long term."

He looked at Katie's beautiful face as she watched him. She was right.

"All I'm asking is, are you staying or going?" she asked calmly.

Derek sat and stared at her phone. He still felt as if Katie didn't truly apologize but brushed over what she'd done. Derek didn't know if Katie understood why he was upset in the first place. It seemed as if the entire situation shifted and he was being given the choice to either stay or leave.

"Don't feel obligated either," she disrupted his thoughts.

Derek looked up at her, then deleted the text thread.

CHAPTER 17

Charlotte, NORTH CAROLINA

PRESENT DAY – 3AM

It never felt good to abruptly wake up out of deep sleep, something Derek experienced several times already in the week. He sat up and quickly began to look around his bedroom. When he realized where he was, he let out a sigh and lay back down. It was rare for him to be unable to sleep, but this was the third night in a row that he could not see a dream through. He was a heavy sleeper, so waking up in the middle of the night was something that he was not used to. Derek reached over and grabbed his phone to see that it was three in the morning. He felt off track and out of alignment. Even when he prayed, it was as if his prayers weren't getting past the ceiling. He called his mother Gloria, unable to think of any better solution. She answered rather quickly, sounding as if she was wide awake. Derek didn't expect her to answer but was glad that she did.

"Hey, I was just checking on y'all," Derek said, unsure of how to start the conversation.

"At two in the morning?" Gloria asked before clearing her throat.

"Who is that?" Derek's grandmother Mattie asked from the background.

"This is Derek, ma," Gloria answered.

"Is he okay?" Mattie asked.

"I'm talking to him now," Gloria yawned into the phone. "Me and your grandma fell asleep in the living room watching TV, so I guess it's good you called. What's up?"

"I can't sleep."

"Oh," Gloria said, relieved. "Did you pray?"

"Yeah, more than once. It's been like this for the last few days."

Derek got up and walked into the living room to sit in the dark on the couch.

"Okay so, what is keeping you up at night?" Gloria asked.

"Nothing that I can think of, I don't know what it is," Derek said.

There was a brief silence over the phone, Gloria wasn't convinced.

"It has to be something if it has you calling here at two in the morning," Gloria said.

"I don't know," Derek said.

Derek then glanced at the small living room table and noticed a black and gold ink pen there. It was an ink pen that belonged to the firm that Katie worked for.

"You know what it is," Gloria said firmly to him. "You already know, no need to keep playing the guessing game."

"I'm not, I— "

"You are. You forget how much I know you," Gloria said.

"I mean, you only raised me for eighteen years, might forget some things," Derek said sarcastically.

"And nine months in my belly—nine long months; don't shortchange me boy," Gloria made Derek smile. "But you won't sleep until you go make that right, whatever happened when you went out there. You say it was fine, but I know it wasn't."

Derek laid down on the couch.

"Ma, I'm not trippin' about it. It was nothing, I let it go," he said to her.

"Did you? Because you are telling me that this week you can't sleep, and since you were a baby, you have always slept like a log. The last time you really couldn't sleep is when your friend got killed."

"I've been working, doing a lot. I just need a vacation," Derek said.

"Stop it," Gloria said. "Don't do that. I've told you since you were little, say what you mean and mean what you say. You need to call her and work whatever this is out."

"Why do I have to do that? She hasn't called me. If that's how she wants it to be then it is what it is," Derek said.

"If I was over there, I would pop you. That's ridiculous. You were just up here talking to me about proposing and now you act like you don't have a care in the world. As excited as you were, I know you care. I know you do," Gloria then blew her nose. "Excuse me."

Derek just listened, he often didn't go back and forth with Gloria. If he was honest with himself, everything that happened in Galveston was heavy on his mind. As much as he tried not to think about it, he failed miserably to do so.

"You will grow old and miserable with regrets being prideful. Do not be that person. You are losing sleep because you aren't at peace about it. You being unable to sleep is probably God talking to you. Stop waiting for her if you don't want it to end. Be a man and go fix it, go make it right," Gloria said to him.

"Amen," Mattie said in the background. "That's right, be a man."

Derek sat up on the couch and let out a sigh as he held the phone up to his ear.

"You right."

"I know," Gloria said. "So, stop fighting it and do what you know you need to do."

Everything that Gloria said was hard for Derek to digest, it went against how he was accustomed to moving most of his young life. It was rare for him to struggle to detach and move on, but in this case he struggled. His mother was right, his pride was what kept him from reaching out. He didn't want to look weak or be taken for granted.

"Sleep on it, decide what man you're going to be, you know I love you either way. I just want you to do what is best for yourself."

After getting off the phone with Gloria, he laid in his bed, still in deep thought. He realized that he needed to be honest with himself, and that would lead him to doing what was the most difficult for himself. Derek prayed for wisdom and guidance; already knowing what he had to do. He swallowed his pride and accepted that there was no way around the path he would have to take.

CHAPTER 18

The work week flew by much faster than usual. The office was quiet and peaceful due to several people out on vacation or working remotely. Derek sat at his desk staring at his two computer monitors in front of him. His mind was elsewhere as it had been for the past few days. His mother Gloria's words still echoed in his mind, and had an idea of what he would do next. A text message from his friends group came to his phone that then was followed by several others:

Are we pullin' up Friday? D I know you are because your girl gon' be there.

The message was from Preston to the rest of the group. Preston also sent a picture of the flyer for Imani Prince's art show. Imani Prince, another one of Katie's best friends, was well known for her ability to draw, paint, and to sculpt clay and create pottery. She extended an invite to everyone she knew and that included Derek's group of friends. As Tone, Elle, and Preston discussed it, Derek ignored the conversation. He had no intention of going, knowing that Katie would be there. He didn't care to be around her friends anyway. Derek got up from his desk and walked over to Chuck's office, Chuck grinned as soon as he saw Derek.

"There he is. I love what I've been seeing from you. Keep it up," Chuck said. "What's up?"

"I wanted to see when the next on-boarding consultations were coming up," Derek said. "I just wanted to get some more hands on experience with being client facing."

"I like the initiative. Might not have any open until next week though," Chuck said as he looked on his computer. "I can let you know if something comes up."

Derek nodded and headed back to his desk. His goal was to stay as busy as possible to keep his mind occupied.

"Hold on," Chuck said, making Derek stop and turnaround. "Three actually came up, but all three are on Friday. You wouldn't be coming back until Saturday. If you are cool with that then you could take one of these."

"Where?" Derek sat down.

Derek was just glad to have a reason not to be around Friday.

"Denver, Phoenix, and Kansas City," Chuck looked up from his computer screen.

Derek had no desire to go to any of the three cities, he contemplated staying home and finding something else to do Friday night. It would just be more difficult to occupy himself while all attention would be on Imani's art show.

"Think on it and get back to me," Chuck told him.

As Derek stood up to walk out, another analyst named Cody rushed into the office.

"Chuck, I can't do Friday's onboard for Anomaly. Kelly may be going into labor," he said.

"It's a major onboard, are you sure? What if we put in an emergency same-day return? It's Dallas, it's always easy to book," Chuck said.

Derek stopped in his tracks when he heard 'Dallas' come out of Chuck's mouth.

"I can't, it's just cutting it too close," Cody said.

"I can do it," Derek said as he walked back into the office.

Cody glanced at Derek then back at Chuck.

"I mean, if Chuck clears it," Cody said as he shrugged. "It would be a huge help."

They both looked at Chuck.

"This is a major new client, it is serious business," Chuck said.

"I can handle it," Derek said confidently.

Cody assured Derek that he could call or text him with any questions or concerns.

"Be on your A-game, this is a big one. You can't fumble it," Chuck told him.

Derek nodded and walked out. He would be headed to Dallas that upcoming Friday, the last place he expected to be headed anytime soon. Apart from the numerous text messages about the art show, he had a text from Troy inviting him out to play basketball after work. Derek met with them after work at a small gym to play a few games. He hadn't spoken to Troy since the two of them went back and forth in Troy's driveway. Much of Derek's frustration was taken out on the basketball court. He played aggressively when he went for lay ups, dunks, and held defense. As usual, the others commented and marveled at how he played. They played basketball for hours and were now completely exhausted. Troy felt accomplished, enduring much longer than the last time they all played.

"I didn't think you would come out," Troy told him afterwards.

"Why wouldn't I? It's always good giving y'all buckets," Derek gave Troy a fist bump.

"I know you saw me out here!" Troy flexed his arms. "I'm gettin' back to the old me!"

"Reach!" someone else yelled, causing them all to laugh.

Troy and Derek lingered outside of the gym to talk as they usually did. Neither of them held any animosity towards one another from their previous conversation despite it becoming escalated. The two of them spoke as if it never happened.

"I'm going back," Derek told him.

Troy finished taking a large gulp from his water bottle as he looked at Derek in confusion.

"Going back in there to play?' Troy asked, pointing back at the gym.

"Back to Texas."

Troy paused, then mouthed 'wow' as he threw his bag in the backseat of his car.

"I think you were right," Derek explained. "I went out there with my mind in the wrong place, trying to prove something to myself."

Troy leaned back against his car; arms crossed as he listened to Derek talk.

"I think I've been motivated by the past and me second guessing myself, always hearing stuff about how lucky I am and all that. I mean, I know I got one, I know," Derek shook his head as Troy laughed.

"So why back to Texas?" Troy asked.

"This will bother me until I deal with it. I was just going to take the L and move on, but I can't. I gotta' talk to this man and see what the problem is. I just know me; it will keep eating me up if I don't go see about it."

Derek was in a much better place mentally compared to the last time he and Troy spoke. As he talked about his plan out loud, he felt better but still uneasy about it.

"Katie know about it?" Troy asked.

"No. I wouldn't tell her anyway."

Troy took a deep breath as he rubbed his chin.

"Man...I don't know," Troy said. "I'm glad you came to terms with why things might have gone left, but this, I don't know. Things got crazy last time, and it's a lot going on with that family."

"I hear you. But if I'm going to have anything with her, ever... I have to handle this. I can't sleep until I do."

Some of the other men suddenly walked out of the gym.

"Y'all still out here?" one of them asked.

They all shook hands with Derek and Troy, giving their farewells. Once they all were at a distance, Troy turned and looked back at Derek.

"You prayed about it? You definitely will need wisdom because this is serious."

"I'm serious too," Derek said to him.

Troy nodded and shook Derek's hand, showing that he had his support.

"Handle it then."

CHAPTER 19

McKinney, TEXAS

BERRY RESIDENCE

The house was once again silent as it had been for the last few days, almost as if the life was taken out of it. It wasn't as vibrant as it usually was, but rather gray, dull, and almost depressing. Tristan and Olivia were upstairs, watching tv, not saying too much of anything. Jared was at one of his friend's houses and would more than likely be home late. Robert and Glenda went back to Muskogee. Walter found himself walking through the house, reminiscing as he looked at pictures on the wall. It was the first time in a long time that he took the time to stop and look at all that he and his family had. He stopped and looked at a family picture that was taken fifteen years prior, right above it was a picture from Walter and Laura's wedding. There was also a picture of Walter and his father on that same wedding day. He began to think back on the early days and realize how far he'd come, from the small house he and Laura had in Houston to the much larger home that they were currently in. Even in his own upbringing, he, Janice, and Jeffrey grew up in Memphis without much of anything. The three of them were only able to make it through academics. Being the smartest and performing the best in school was the only way that any of them were able to attend college.

As he made his way upstairs, the sound of the tv in the master bedroom could be heard. Laura was in bed watching a movie while at the same time glancing at her phone. Walter noticed that Laura was texting back and forth with her sister Mel. When she saw Walter, she extended her arm out towards him, despite still being focused on the tv.

"Where were you?" she asked.

Walter walked over and sat on the floor next to Laura's side of the bed. Laura then rested her hand on Walter's chest after reaching down to hug him.

"I was just downstairs thinking," Walter said.

"Hold on, hold on," Laura held her index finger up, still focused on the TV.

Once the commercial break came, Laura then gave Walter her full attention.

"Sorry, this is better than I thought it would be."

Walter shook his head, grinning.

"I was sitting downstairs thinking about a lot of things," Walter said again.

"You were downstairs just thinking? In silence?" Laura winced. "That sounds depressing."

She and Walter both laughed.

"Just...with everything from this past weekend, my mind has been everywhere," Walter continued, massaging Laura's hand.

"It was a lot," Laura said. "One thing I'll say is I see why you are not quick to invite Janice places. I didn't know she could instigate and stir up things like that."

Walter hadn't spoken to Janice since he saw her that past weekend. She called Laura to check on her, but didn't speak to Walter.

"You know, when you collapsed, it shook me."

"I know, Mel and daddy made it known how shook you were."

Laura could tell by Walter's demeanor that he was coming from a place of sincerity.

"I thought about losing you...what would I do?" Walter asked. "It just started to put some things into perspective for me, made me really understand and value you all. I need to start cherishing everyday with you and the kids."

As Walter talked, Laura rubbed the top of Walter's head, comforting him.

"Those were the first thoughts that came into my head," Walter turned around onto his knees, still holding Laura's hand.

"I'm glad," Laura said. "We're always here in your corner. We are a team to the end. Make sure you know that."

"I do," Walter said. "I get it now."

"We don't need Walter Berry the executive who went to a major school and has all of this corporate clout. I need my husband, and the kids need their daddy. All of this made me understand and really put into perspective why you are the way that you are at times. As I laid here and thought about it, and how you came up, I get it. But me and the kids don't have the situation that your mom, you, Janice, and Jeffrey had, so adjust a little."

"I sat Jared down before he left, had a long talk with him, let him know where I blew it. And he opened up to me, talked to me, we made plans. I felt like I accomplished more just in that conversation than I have all of these years," Walter smiled. "I should be better than this. Pathetic huh?"

"Stop it," Laura grabbed Walter's cheeks. "Nothing pathetic about making things right.

Everything starts from now. What are you going to do about our oldest?"

Walter's smile began to fade.

"I don't know," he said. "I'm sure she doesn't want anything to do with me."

"So?" Laura said strongly with an attitude.

"So? What can I do? She may not ever talk to me again, and I'm not going to try and force her to. She's a grown woman who thinks I've been against her most of her life, her mind is made up."

Laura rolled her eyes, readjusting her head scarf.

"I don't care if she sidesteps you a million times; you better try a million and one. You need to show some effort," Laura grabbed a small bottle of water out of the mini-fridge next to their nightstand. "Swallow that pride."

"I'm supposed to keep hitting my head against a brick wall and keep calling her for her to ignore me? She is not going to answer," Walter said.

"Call?" Laura asked in disgust. "Are you serious?"

Laura got face to face with Walter.

"She was in person when you ran her out of here, and she made the effort to come home knowing that you two weren't on the best terms. And you sit up here talking about calling her? You know what you have to do."

Walter knew that Laura was right, and it was clear that she wasn't budging on it.

"I'm too old to be sleeping on the couch," he said quietly to himself.

Walter then pulled out his laptop and prepared himself to book a flight to Charlotte.

CHAPTER 20

Charlotte, NORTH CAROLINA.
AIRPORT.

The anxiety that Derek experienced Friday morning was one he never experienced before a client visit, but it had nothing to do with the client visit. He sat constantly second-guessing himself and wondering if what he planned was the way to go. The anxiety intensified when he sent Katie a text message that morning, trying to extend an olive branch. Katie read it and didn't respond to it. Derek told his mother Gloria his plan, she was a little skeptical about it but was more so distracted by the original intention for her call.

"Your aunt Valerie's house got ran in last night, about two in the morning. Somebody tried to rob them," Gloria told him.

Gloria didn't have a bit of concern in her voice when she told him. Derek, while surprised by the news, wasn't worried about his aunt or his father. There wasn't much that his father Maurice or his aunt

Valerie were afraid of, and they knew how to hold their own.

"Yeah, we're okay," Valerie told Derek when he called to check on them. "There were two of them that busted in, well one through the door and the other through a window. I'm a light sleeper so as soon as I heard the window collapse, I grabbed my gun. Before I could even get up, I heard four shots go off. I think Maurice hit one of them."

"Glad y'all are good, that's crazy," Derek said.

"Yeah, I just hope it wasn't one of these kids we know from one of the other neighborhoods. Hold on."

Maurice got on the phone and explained it almost the same as Valerie explained it. He was a little more talkative than Derek was used to.

"I'm glad you don't have to deal with this," Maurice said to Derek.

"What you mean? That could happen anywhere," Derek said.

"Yeah, but a lot of this is BS coming back to bite me years later. I'm just glad you never got sucked into it when you lived here. I'd be hopeless, man."

"What you mean?" Derek asked.

"Listen. I'm serious," Maurice said. "I already know I ain' have a lot to do with it, but you the best thing that I have produced in this life man. I hear about what you got going and how you are living, and I know if somebody like my son can come from me, I got hope to be a better person at some point. So, keep being you and doing you, don't ever change."

Derek was shocked at what he was told. His dad never said anything like that to him, and it was rare for him to be as open as he was. He didn't know how to respond. Their call ended shortly after as Derek's flight to Dallas began to board. After hearing what Maurice said, all of Derek's doubts were gone. He felt a sudden wave of confidence and was convinced that he was doing was the right thing. Derek landed in Dallas a little after noon central standard time. The meeting for onboarding the new client was scheduled for 2pm. He was taken aback when his cab driver pulled up to the client site, a tall glass building that looked like a large diamond on the middle of the city when the sun shined on it. Every single story was floor to ceiling double sided windows.

"What is this place?" Derek asked his counterpart Joe that he was working with. "This building is crazy."

"Oh yeah, Anomaly Automation is a major company and has grown quite a bit," Joe said. "We may meet a lot of their c-suite executives so just be prepared for that."

Joe was very calm, humble, and relaxed, something that Derek wasn't used to. Before long,

Derek and Joe were approached and greeted by two men who would then escort them. One of the men was one of the network administrators and the other was the director of technology for Anomaly. As they made their way down the long hall to the elevators, Derek couldn't help but to observe the environment. All of the employees at Anomaly moved with urgency and intention. The floor that they went to was full of cubicles, a person sitting in each one focused on the computer screen in front of them. There were no side conversations or any conversations at all for that matter. It was as if they were robots, something that made Derek uneasy. Seeing how the employees at Anomaly worked made him a little more appreciative of his job.

"Here comes the CEO and the CFO," Joe said to Derek as they walked down another hallway.

Derek looked to see two men walking down the hall towards them, followed by three women carrying laptops, two of them were on their cell phones. One of the two men was a few inches shorter than the other and had a cold-blooded stare as he looked in Derek and Joe's direction.

"Gentlemen, hello," the man said. A sudden smile crossed his face as he shook all their hands and introduced himself. "I hope these two are making the most of your time."

"They are, Mr. London, but of course we are here to help you all," Joe said to him.

"You don't have to call me Mr. London; Matt will do just fine. Excuse me, my apologies, this is Whitney, our CFO," Matt said as Whitney stepped forward and shook everyone's hand.

Whitney was taller than Matt and seemed to be much more of a gentle spirit than the others. Matt fully explained how important the situation was and how much he was invested in the security measures that they purchased.

"I'll let you all get back to it. I just wanted to greet you and say we are taking this seriously. Enough has been taken out of this place without our stamp of approval, so that stops now on all fronts," Matt told them. "Too many assets compromised."

Matt pat Derek on the back before walking away. As he walked away, Whitney followed close behind him like a lap dog, followed by the three women glued to their phones and speaking amongst themselves. While the on-boarding session continued, Derek couldn't help but to think about what his course of action would be once they were finished. He vaguely remembered where Katie's parents lived. Derek didn't even know if Walter would be home, all he could do was hope and pray. Derek had to think even faster since the on-board session was complete an hour later, much faster than he anticipated. He and Joe debriefed in the lobby.

"Pretty straight to the point huh?" Joe asked with a smile on his face.

"Very, I've never had a session go that quickly," Derek said, putting his notebook into his bag.

"Yeah, usually big spenders know what they want and get straight to it. Not much time for small talk," Joe said, smiling again. "Now are you based out of Charlotte too with Cody?"

"Yes sir. I fly back tonight. Flight doesn't leave until ten, though," Derek said.

"Geez, you have a lot of time to kill," Joe said, concerned.

"I have people out here, so I'll be good," Derek said, making Joe relieved.

Derek was trying to end the conversation sooner than later; he didn't care to have small talk and he had a lot of things he needed to figure out. But Joe was kind to him so he had more patience for him.

"Well," Joe threw his bag over his shoulder and extended his hand out to shake Derek's hand. "You did great today; it was nice meeting you and best of luck to you Derek."

Once Joe left, Derek began to walk around the lobby trying to figure out what his next move would be. He didn't have much time.

"How do I get out here and not even know where the house is?" Derek said to himself as he shook his head.

He pulled out his phone and began to look through it, trying to come up with an idea of how he was going to get to Katie's parents' house. Derek turned around to head towards the doors to go outside but immediately stopped in his tracks. Across the lobby stood Walter Berry, staring directly at him.

CHAPTER 21

Walter was glad to be leaving work early. He did all that needed to be done and was now ready to get home. There were several things he needed to figure out for the weekend, which was where his mind was most of the day. Walking into the lobby to see his daughter's boyfriend Derek stunned him; it was the only thing that threw his thoughts off the rails the entire day. When Derek turned around and the two of them made eye contact, it erased all doubt. Walter glanced at his watch, then slowly walked towards Derek. He noticed Derek's collared shirt tucked into his business slacks and the messenger bag hanging on his shoulder, which let Walter know that Derek had to be there on business. Once Walter got close, Derek turned around to stand face to face with him.

"What are you doing here?" Walter asked.

"Working. We just had an onboard consultation for Anomaly," Derek said.

There were so many thoughts and emotions flowing through Derek as he stood in front of Walter.

"You work here?" Derek asked.

"You could say that," Walter said carelessly. "You travel for work I'm guessing?"

"Yeah," Derek looked around, then looked back at Walter. "But I was actually looking for you."

Walter's eyes widened, "Looking for me?"

Derek nodded; eyes still locked on Walter. Walter knew he needed to somehow break the tension; the way Derek stared at him made him uncomfortable. He didn't know what to expect, or if Derek was going to make a scene.

"You ate yet?" Walter asked.

Derek agreed to go and eat with him. Walter knew that the last interaction between the two of them was everything but pleasant, so he wanted to extend an olive branch to at least be respectful.

"This seems like a good company to work for. I bet it's hard to get into this place," Derek said as they walked to the car.

"Looks can be deceiving," Walter said.

The car ride was silent apart from the small bits of small talk every few moments. Derek was the last person that Walter expected to have in his car. The two of them ended up at an upscale steakhouse. Just from the ambiance, Derek knew that it was an expensive restaurant. The menu confirmed it for him once they sat at their table.

"Hello Mr. Berry! We haven't seen you in a while! How are you?" The hostess greeted Walter as the waiter sat two glasses of water on the table.

She was thrilled to see him. She was an older white woman, much shorter than both Walter and Derek. After the small talk, she rattled off Walter's order to him to confirm it. He didn't have to open the menu once.

"You are always on it, that's exactly right," he said, smiling at her.

Derek ordered one of the cheapest meals on the menu.

"Get what you want, don't be modest," Walter told him.

"I'm good, but I appreciate it," Derek said as he handed his menu to the waiter.

There was once again a moment of silence between the two of them, Walter could see Derek wrestling with if he was going to speak first or just keep quiet. But Walter was tired of the silence.

"Might as well get to it right?" Walter took off his suit jacket. "The last time we saw each other, it was hostile. How I handled that wasn't right. I do apologize, from one man to another."

Derek's eyebrows raised. The apology was more than he had expected, but less than he needed.

"But what is it?" Derek asked.

"What?"

"What is the problem that you have with me? I plan to make things with Katie official. As much as I don't want issues with you, I'm going to do it regardless. So, we either squash whatever this is here, or it's just gonna' be what it is."

It took a lot for Walter to have this conversation, especially since he rarely explained himself to anyone. It was even more of a challenge to sit across from Derek, who he still felt disrespected by. But Walter also couldn't help but to think that all of it was meant to happen. What were the odds of him running into Derek in the lobby of his job? In Walter's mind, that could not be a coincidence. Telling himself that all of it was happening for a reason gave him the motivation to be open and make things right.

"You already know that my daughter and I are not on the best of terms, as we haven't been for years now. When you came here with her, you ate in my house, slept in my house, showered in my house, the whole nine, yet simply followed her lead. You made our problems your problems and acted that out. She probably told you the worst of the worst about me. I get it. But to come where I live and do that is a different level of disrespect, I don't respect that."

"She never talked about you," Derek said. "I always had to bring you up. I never knew y'all had issues going back years. She never told me. I'm protective over her, so that night it was just second nature to defend her."

"But you read something in her journal I'm sure," Walter said vaguely as the two waiters appeared to sit their entrees down on the table.

"What do you mean?"

"The journal, Katie's book. The blue leather one with the red ribbon," Walter smirked as he looked at Derek's startled face. "I walked past the guest room, and you were sleep with that journal across your chest. Hopefully you got a good look at it because I never have, my wife always kept me from it."

Derek was hesitant to answer.

"I only know of a few times the two of you butted heads when she was in high school, and how she felt about you sometimes. That and her ex lingering around because you liked him."

Walter knew Derek took a jab at him with the comment about Katie's ex-boyfriend.

"Me and Katie hadn't spoken in almost five years before you two came," Walter said.

Derek's eyes once again widened.

"If you want the truth, I always thought of you as the one she was using to spite me. All the times she would call my wife to brag about you and speak so highly of you, and everything she used to say to describe you, I used to be for her. She was always my baby girl, man, always. I gave her the world but never shielded her from how ugly it is. Then of course as you just said, her last boyfriend Isaac always reached out even when the two of them were done. He was how I found out about you, not Katie, even though I never told her or my wife that."

Derek was in complete disbelief at what he heard. All of it was new to him and helped him connect the dots on many things.

"I stayed in contact with him to keep up with Katie. I knew he always checked on her so I would get information from him. So, when you came into the picture, I knew about it. Isaac would passively talk down on you, even though he tried to mask it as being concerned about Katie. He always acted like he was concerned if you were good for her just based on some social media stuff and other things. I should have known it was stupid then. I let his opinion twist my view of you before I could even meet you. Ironic now that I think about it because I just said I couldn't respect you for that same thing. I thought you were just the typical young dude I see these days looking for the easy way through life and found a good girl to carry you along."

Derek began to think back on the argument he and Katie had, realizing that his anger was misplaced the entire time.

"I wanted to believe the negative about you. I didn't want to believe Katie's words about you, didn't want to believe she was doing fine without me. My daughter is a younger me, strong willed, determined, and when she didn't do things I wanted or how I thought she should, it was a war. I wasn't making time for her but at the same time tried to control her."

Walter and Derek both took some time to eat. Walter said a lot, most of which he never verbalized to anyone before. He felt that he needed to sort his thoughts in preparation to speak with Katie, which he knew would not be easy. Walter also felt a little remorseful about his first interaction with Derek, especially after finding out that Derek was not aware of the situation.

"At the end of the day, you came into the picture at a rough time, you just got caught in the middle. But I respect you for how you stood up for Katie. I respect that, and having this conversation with me takes a lot of courage," Walter nodded. "Not sure how you would have found me if I didn't see you in that lobby."

They both laughed at Walter's comment.

"I was trying to figure it out," Derek continued to laugh.

"Then, what would you had done if I was out of town?"

"I would have just chalked it up as a work trip I guess," Derek said. "We got a lot cleared up though. I'm glad we had this convo, man to man. Are we good now though? Like really good?"

Walter reached out and shook Derek's hand to signify that all was behind them and there was no longer an issue between them.

"It may not be believable after all of this, but I do want what's best for Katie. I love her more than anything."

"And I do too," Derek told him. "I came on the trip to meet you and to get your blessing. The old me wouldn't have cared to do that, but with her, I wanted to do this the right way. She won't say it, but I know it's important to her too."

"I would hope so," Walter said.

"You need to tell her, no point in this beef continuing on," Derek insisted.

"She was able to go years without speaking to me," Walter looked down at his phone. "I don't think me going to her now is going to move her."

He sent a text earlier to Laura explaining how he ran into Derek. She responded to him in excitement, typing in all caps and with exclamation marks.

"My wife is going crazy," Walter grinned. "I told her I was with you. She loves you."

"How is she doing? Is she okay?" Derek asked.

"She is, the doctors still don't know what happened. None of us do, it's crazy."

Walter agreed to take Derek to the airport once they left the restaurant, but first took him to the Berry household to see Laura. The ride there was much more interactive than their ride to the restaurant was. It felt surreal for Derek to be in the Berry home without Katie being there with him. When Laura saw Derek, she gave him a long tight hug with a big smile on her face, genuinely happy to see him.

"Jared will be mad that he wasn't here, he really took to you but he's out with friends. It's so good to see you again!"

Derek felt at home when interacting with Laura, she truly knew how to make someone feel welcomed. Walter walked over and stood behind Laura as she sat on the arm of the couch.

"I know this is the last place you probably expected to be!" Laura made them all laugh.

"He wants to take our daughter from us," Walter made Laura to frown in confusion as she looked back at him.

"Take her away?" Laura asked.

Walter held his hand up and pointed to the black wedding band on his ring finger. Laura's eyes widened and she turned to Derek, who blushed with a nervous smile on his face.

"That's what you want?" Laura asked.

Derek nodded in response; a nervous grin on his face.

"Hello? I can't hear you, don't get nervous on me now!" Laura yelled dramatically.

"Yes ma'am," Derek's grin turned into a full-blown smile.

Laura and Walter then turned and looked at one another, speaking without speaking. The two of them knew each other well enough to communicate solely through their expressions.

"I'm good," Walter told Laura. "Him being willing to come to me and discuss our problems man to man shows me a lot."

Laura didn't respond, she looked back over at Derek. Although she still had a slight grin on her face, Derek knew that she was no longer in a lighthearted playful mood.

"I love my daughter Derek, more than myself. I'll kill over her," Laura said, eyes locked on Derek. "That's my firstborn, my baby. You better take care of her."

"I love her too, and of course I will," Derek said.

"Okay then, because we'll be family. It will be much easier for me to beat you down if you don't," Laura smiled, once again lightening the mood.

"Yes ma'am."

Laura then stood up and gave Derek another hug.

"I wouldn't want it to be anyone else but you," she said as she hugged him.

Olivia then began yelling for Laura from upstairs.

"Auntie Mel is on the phone for you!" Olivia yelled.

"Girl, what did I tell you about answering my—" Laura began to make her way towards the stairs, then quickly turned around. "If I don't come back down, I'll see you soon...son-in-law."

Walter watched Laura as she ran up the stairs, then turned to Derek, who tried to hold his smile back. Derek hadn't felt as good as he did in that moment in a long time.

"Well…" Walter held his hand out and shook Derek's hand. "There you have it. Good thing we worked it out, huh?"

"For sure," Derek said. "Make sure you come down for the proposal in two months."

"You'll be seeing me much sooner than that," Walter said. "More like tomorrow."

"Tomorrow?"

"You came here to make amends. Time for me to go make some too," Walter said.

"That will mean a lot to her."

"We're about to find out…"

CHAPTER 22

Charlotte, NORTH CAROLINA
FRIDAY.

Exhaustion was an understatement for Katie Berry; she hadn't had much sleep in the past few days. She was glad that she took the day off to rest, having stayed up until 4am. The past week was one of the busiest weeks she'd had in a long time, having friends in town didn't make it any easier. As Katie lay on the coach with her laptop resting on her torso, her close friend Imani Prince walked out of the bedroom in a bathrobe, hair wrapped in a towel. She picked up her phone to check her messages and social media. Imani was taller than the average woman, she played volleyball and ran track most of her life. She and Katie grew close during their freshman year at Darcy, so the two of them knew each other very well. Often, Katie would tell people that Imani knew her too well.

"Sabrina still sleeping?" Imani asked.

"Yeah, she was up the latest and had a little too much," Katie said, eyes still locked on her laptop screen.

"Did Paris land yet?" Imani asked. "She hasn't texted me."

"I haven't heard from her, but Bianca will be bringing her from the airport."

Katie's attention was divided between her laptop and her phone. She had several text messages coming in from the group she had created for the members of the hospitality team. Family and Friends Day was coming up in addition to Joint Sunday fellowship, which would both be on the same Sunday. Family and Friends Day was when members were urged to invite at least three people to accompany them. Joint Sunday was when a sister church in the city would come and have joint service together with them, so Katie had her hands full. She didn't feel like working in Tasha's place anymore, she just wanted to hand it all over to everyone else and be left alone. As Katie delegated responsibilities in the group message, Sabrina walked out of Bianca's bedroom, still in the volleyball shorts and t-shirt she slept in.

"She's alive!" Imani grinned as she sat in front of Katie's body length mirror.

Sabrina collapsed onto the couch and clung to Katie as if she was a child clinging to her mother. She slept in Bianca's room since Bianca wasn't home the night before.

"I am so tired, and so hungry," Sabrina said.

"Y'all trying to go eat somewhere?" Imani asked.

"Umm no," Katie said and shook her head.

"Definitely not, I can barely move right now," Sabrina co-signed.

Bianca then walked through the front door to greet everyone followed by Paris Irvin, another one of Katie's closest friends. Paris had an energetic and lively personality, so much so that she could take all the energy out of a room when she walked in. Paris came in and gave everyone hugs, she had a huge smile and it always stood out how perfect her teeth were. Several people used to joke that they had to be fake, and some even took the rumor that they were fake and ran with it. Imani's relaxed monotone voice quickly changed to be more energetic to match the energy that Paris had.

While Katie, Sabrina, Imani, and Paris were a tight knit group of friends, Paris and Imani were closer to each other than to anyone else. Bianca had her own circles of friends but occasionally would spend time with Katie and her friends. Paris and Imani were both from Detroit and after graduation from college, Paris moved to Atlanta and Imani moved to Washington D.C. The two of them knew each other since the seventh grade but became close friends in high school. Although the four of them wanted the best for one another, there was always unspoken competition and comparison amongst the four of them. It was that way since college and amplified once they all graduated. Katie hated it, she felt that because she was the only one of the four that came from a well-off family, a lot of the competition was aimed at her.

All of them relaxed much of the afternoon before they had to get ready for Imani's art exhibit. They ordered food and sat in the living room and streamed TV shows to watch.

"Umm Katherine, is Derek coming tonight?" Paris asked as she put a few chicken wings on her plate.

"Not sure yet, but if his friends are there, you know he will be," Katie said.

"Oh okay, I mean I don't care, I was just curious. Ryan is only going to the Atlanta one so it's not a big deal anyway," Paris said.

Ryan was Paris' husband.

"How are y'all?" Paris continued. "You don't even talk about him like that no more."

"I know right! I was just thinking that," Imani agreed.

"We are good," Katie forced a smile. "No complaints."

"Well that's good. We thought you ran him off," Paris said.

"Oop," Imani's eyes widened, covering her mouth.

"Run him off?" Katie asked, rolling her eyes. "Girl be quiet."

"I'm just saying, you know you were a bit of a pit bull for a while!" Paris made them all laugh when she began to growl like a dog.

Katie let out a fake laugh then rolled her eyes again, irritated by the comment.

"Hold on, did you basically just call me a—"

"Aht aht! Redacted!" Sabrina yelled.

"I'm just messing with you, girl," Paris smiled. "You probably next up; we thought you'd be right after us."

"Right?" Imani agreed.

Both Paris and Imani were married, having met their husbands at Darcy. They'd been married for four years but had known their husbands for much longer.

"I don't care, I'm not on a time crunch. I don't even think about it," Katie brushed their statements off.

"I'm just saying like... you got a lot going for yourself, you fine, it should be a no-brainer, right?" Paris asked everyone.

"Well dang thanks y'all!" Sabrina interjected, causing them all to burst out into laughter.

Imani and Paris began to compliment her and explain what they were trying to say. Katie looked down at a text from Bianca:

She is annoying...I can't...and poor Sabrina...maybe if she got those edges together chile...

Katie looked up to see Bianca in the kitchen doing a small happy dance as she ate, which she usually did whenever she got some food. Katie began to mouth 'I hate you' to her. Bianca didn't care to be around Katie's friends because she was often annoyed by all of them. *You are nothing like them,* she once told Katie.

"Anyway!" Paris yelled over everyone, "I was just saying I was surprised KB hasn't been locked down yet. You always have these super serious relationships I thought you would be locked down."

"Serious as in not letting other people hit while in a relationship? That's just being faithful girl," Katie made them all laugh and scream again.

"Ohh, is that what we are doing today?" Paris continued to laugh.

While Katie came off as kidding, she wasn't. Her patience was low with her friends and they hadn't caught on to it yet. Jokes and slick remarks didn't usually get under Katie's skin, but she wasn't in the mood.

"I mean, if you're doing you out here that's cool too, just don't slip up and have kids running around by a bum like some people," Imani said slyly, causing Paris' mouth to dramatically drop. "Let me stop, Lord forgive me."

Imani's statement pressed another button for Katie because of the obvious jab that was taken at Miah, Sabrina and Bianca picked up on it by Katie's reaction.

"What do you mean by that?" Katie looked up at Imani, moving her laptop to the side.

"So, what's the plan for tonight y'all?" Sabrina stepped in to change the subject.

Sabrina could feel the tension in the room; she was often the mediator whenever situations arose. Katie glanced back towards Bianca again, whose eyebrows were raised and a smirk on her face. She simply bit into the slice of pizza that she held as she watched everyone else. Katie knew that her mood was not the best and needed to check it before it got worse. It started with Derek sending her a dry text that morning after having not heard from him all week. She felt herself thinking and feeling like the old her, something that she did not want. After feeling sad earlier in the week about what happened with her father and with Derek, her feelings quickly evolved into frustration and anger. She was tired of feeling down, so she didn't care to hear about her dad, Derek, or anyone else that was on the wrong side of her. In her mind, trying to be the bigger person and extend grace didn't work, so she felt she had the right to embrace the old way just a little.

As the evening rolled in, Katie and her friends dressed to impress. Imani had a make-up artist and hairdresser come by to do their makeup and hair; she wanted their makeup to be dramatic to go along with the artistic theme of the night. They all looked amazing based on the comments and attention they received from their pictures and videos on social media. Despite Katie's rough week, she couldn't deny that she enjoyed getting dressed up and taking pictures. She was reminded of why the women that she was with were her friends.

Imani's art show was held at a rooftop lounge, which was laid out beautifully. She left the others much earlier to assist with the set up. There were displays with pottery and figures that Imani sculpted herself, as well as many of her paintings and drawings. The program that attendees received when they came in had a long bio about Imani which was written by Katie. The art show also consisted of an open bar and a table full of desserts and refreshments. All expenses for the show were covered by Imani's husband, who was a very successful sports agent. Her husband was also able to get a few of his clients to advertise the show for Imani. Katie enjoyed herself more as the night went on, but her enjoyment wasn't enough to block out the nagging thoughts of Derek.

"I can't get over how beautiful this is," Paris told Sabrina.

The two of them walked towards Katie, drinks from the bar in their hands.

"You didn't get a drink?" Paris asked Katie.

"No, I'm good right now," Katie said. "I'm loving the dark backgrounds; they really changed this place around."

Imani then walked up to them, so happy. It was the first time they had the chance to see her since earlier in the day. They continued to compliment her and tell her how amazing everything was. Another huge smile came across Imani's face as she spotted someone that was walking up behind Katie. Katie turned around to see Preston and Elliot walking towards them. Her heart immediately sped up when she saw the two of them.

"Good to see you all! Thank you for coming!" Imani hugged them in excitement. "Where is the rest of your crew?"

"Tone is at the bar and you know Derek out of town," Preston said glancing at Katie, who tried to play off her look of surprise.

"Out of town?" Paris also glanced at Katie.

"He travels for work," Katie said.

"Oh, I see," Paris nodded, then shrugged.

Preston nodded towards the food table as Tone walked over, he and Elliot followed him there. Katie's mind began to wander as she stood with her friends. Derek never took travel assignments on Fridays, which in her mind, showed that Derek wanted to avoid seeing her. The thought of that possibility hurt her.

"Oh, here comes your man," Paris said as she took a drink and turned around.

The other two looked behind Katie then looked over at Paris. Katie felt a sense of nervousness but also a sense of relief. A grin streaked its way across her face. She braced herself, thinking about all that she would say and how she would say it. Katie then turned around to see Isaac Duke standing there looking at her.

CHAPTER 23

All of the guests gave a thunderous applause after Imani finished a short speech that eloquently explained what art meant to her, to culture, and to society. It was a speech that Katie wrote a good bit of. Imani ended it with her own heartfelt message of thankfulness toward everyone who attended. Katie, although enjoying herself, was ready to go home. After Imani's speech, Katie walked outside onto the balcony of the lounge where there weren't too many people. The temperature outside was perfect. As she stood holding one of the railings, she closed her eyes and let out a deep breath.

"Hiding out here?"

Katie recognized the voice instantly and turned around to see Isaac behind her. Isaac looked much different than the last time Katie had seen him: bald head and a long, full beard, also very well-dressed. Isaac always could dress well; but now he had the money to buy the expensive clothes to match his keen sense of style.

"I'm not hiding, I just came to get some air," Katie said.

Isaac stood beside her, enjoying with Katie the scenic view from the balcony.

"All of this space out here and you chose to stand right here. Wow," Katie said, making Isaac laugh.

"It's like that? Why so hostile love?" Isaac turned and looked at her.

"What do you want? Why did you come out here?" Katie asked.

"Stop acting like we not cool," Isaac said firmly. "We always been friends, so stop acting brand new on me."

Isaac turned around and leaned back against the rail, his back towards the view.

"We're not friends," Katie said. "Exes don't need to be friends, not at all."

"Your man told you that huh?" Isaac shook his head. "I'm surprised he let you come out here by yourself."

"He's out of town for work."

Katie winced after she responded. She hated that she gave Isaac a response. He nodded as if impressed by Katie's answer.

"I'm happy for him, traveling for work. Grown man moves," Isaac said. "What does he do?"

Katie didn't respond. She knew Isaac too well and knew when he was being sarcastic.

"Glad you're happy. Nice talking to you," Katie began to walk off.

"Hold up, for real," Isaac stopped her from walking back in. "I came out here to talk to you. For real."

"About what?"

"Just...you know, catch up. We used to talk all the time. I'm making sure you good."

The difficult part about dealing with Isaac was that he knew Katie just as well as she knew him. Katie didn't respond, looking past Isaac off into the distance.

"You a little tense," Isaac said calmly. "He must not be putting in work at home. Alright let me chill," Isaac chuckled when Katie frowned. "I know I'm probably not the first person you would hit up, but you can still get at me."

Katie had no desire or energy to go back and forth; usually she would have shut Isaac down and ended the conversation.

"I'm just tired. I need a break, a vacation, something," Katie said, finally making eye contact with Isaac.

"Where you trying to go? Let's book it," Isaac said, excited to pull out his phone.

"You really think I'm going on a vacation with you?"

"Me, you, and some people from school. It doesn't have to be a one-on-one situation," Isaac said.

Katie laughed in his face.

"You really trying to take me somewhere knowing I'm in a relationship," Katie said.

"Then where he taking you?" Isaac asked. "Better yet, where he at right now? My bad, you already said he out of town for work."

"Why am I even talking to you?" Katie turned once again to walk away.

"Because you want to," Isaac grabbed her arm, turning her back around. "What are the odds of you being here alone and I happen to be here? He could have been here with you for all I knew. I wasn't planning on coming here tonight, but something told me to pull up."

"Just… stop," Katie said.

She glanced at the door to see people preparing to leave and Imani taking a few last-minute pictures with guests and sponsors.

"I don't believe in coincidences and you don't either; we always both believed that everything happens for a reason. You know God don't make mistakes," Isaac said.

Isaac's statement confirmed for Katie that he was playing mind games. Isaac wasn't the most religious or spiritual person, and often more skeptical than most.

"All I'm saying is, I know you got your little situation. I just want you to remember how much I was there for you and how much we both made it through," Isaac said.

"And what you put me through."

Isaac nodded without hesitation, sighing.

"I was a wild one, not gon' lie!" he laughed, causing Katie to let out a small laugh. "I'm here until tomorrow night. All I'm saying is that it would be cool to catch up. No pressure. We'll link up, cool?"

Isaac began to back away, making his exit. Katie didn't respond, then let out a deep breath and hung her head. The sound of heels against the ground caused her to lift her head, Sabrina was walking toward her. There was much that Sabrina wanted to say but decided to keep it to herself. She came out on the balcony to get Katie so that they could leave, their driver was downstairs waiting on them.

During the drive home, everyone talked about the art show, Imani was very excited that her first show was a success. Sabrina, Paris, and Imani were the most excited, Katie and Bianca were mellow and laid back. Bianca became a laxed person when she drank. By the time they made it back to the apartment, they'd already decided that they would be going out that night. As they changed clothes to go to a club, Paris was on video chat with her husband to show what she would be wearing that night.

"You not paying attention, look!" Paris pleaded with him.

"I am looking, it's nice," her husband, Ryan, said.

Ryan was clearly distracted, causing Paris to roll her eyes.

"Let me get this call. I'll hit you right back baby," he said before disconnecting the video chat.

It was clear that Paris was bothered although she tried to mask it. She then went into her suitcase and grabbed another outfit, taking off what she had on initially. As they got dressed, Katie sat on the couch next to Bianca, still in her outfit from the art show.

"You keeping that on or you changing?" Sabrina asked Katie.

Katie shook her head, "I'm not going, I'm—"

Katie stopped when Paris suddenly re-emerged in a new outfit, grabbing everyone's attention. Paris had on a short tight skirt and a mesh crop top that was very easy to see through.

"You wearing that? With that? Like that?" Sabrina asked, eyes widened as she looked Paris up and down.

"Dressed like she tryna' catch some," Bianca chimed in.

"Is Ryan cool with you in that?" Katie asked.

"He don't control me my baby. If he cared, maybe he would show it," Paris said dismissively, turning to look at Katie. "Why are you acting brand new?"

"I just wanna' chill, I'm tired," Katie said.

Paris rolled her eyes.

"You used to come out with us all the time," Imani said.

"Right, it's time to get on somebody son tonight," Paris said. "This is what I meant earlier, you are either running people off or closed off period."

Paris began to look at herself on the camera on her phone and snap pictures of herself.

"I don't need to meet new people...for the millionth time. I have someone, I'm good," Katie said, frustrated.

Katie didn't care to keep her composure much longer, Paris got on her nerves ever since she touched down.

"Do you?" Paris asked strongly. "Because just a few hours ago, you didn't even know where your man was. You found out like we found out sis, so how that work?"

Paris often became confrontational when she drank.

"Do you just want people to be as miserable as you?" Katie asked.

"Ooh," Sabrina stepped aside and immediately sat down.

Everyone's eyes widened at Katie's question. Bianca stared at Paris, anxiously awaiting a reply.

"Miserable?" Paris frowned.

Imani also frowned as she turned from the living room mirror and looked at Katie.

"Really though?" Imani said as she rolled her eyes.

"Only person that's miserable is you," Paris said. "You are so used to being the one with the upper hand, having more than everyone else, and now that people are doing well and maybe even better than you, you can't handle it."

Katie's mouth dropped; it was the most ridiculous thing that she'd heard about herself. She looked over at Bianca who shrugged in confusion. They both chuckled.

"What are you talking – you know what I don't care. There has always been this little competition you have had with me for years and it's dumb. You just try to look a way to impress other people and you do too," Katie looked over at Imani.

"You really trying it!" Paris yelled, clapping her hands as she spoke. "All of a sudden everybody wants to be you? Because you got it together, right?"

"I'm not acting like I have it all together. That's what you hoes do, lie for the internet and for other people. Y'all even try to flex with your marriages online and not even good there," Katie said. "Yet y'all wanna' throw shots?"

Paris suddenly aggressively darted towards Katie, clear anger across her face. Bianca quickly shot up from the couch and stepped in front of Katie, pushing Paris back. Bianca then kicked her heels off, bracing herself. Paris regained her composure and signaled for Imani to follow her out the door so they could head to the club. Sabrina was hesitant as she glanced back and forth between Katie and Paris.

"Go on, get out with them," Bianca shooed Sabrina out the door.

Once they left, Bianca then turned to Katie.

"I never liked her, she can't come back here," Bianca said.

Bianca sat next to Katie and put her arm around her as she buried her face in her palms.

"I feel like I'm losing everybody," Katie hugged Bianca.

Bianca didn't do well in moments where a person needed to be consoled or comforted. She always felt awkward in those types of situations. She tried her best to cheer Katie up, but didn't want to get too deep into it.

"Anybody you lose...wasn't for you," Bianca said. "And I'm still here, always. Let's go eat, I'm paying."

Katie simply nodded.

"I'll drive too, see all you gotta' do is ride along. Some great cousin you have!" Bianca smiled as she stood up to go change.

"Drive? You been drinking," Katie said.

"Trust me, my buzz is just about gone."

Although Katie smiled on the outside, she felt down on the inside. Katie truly felt that everything was going left on her and didn't know what to do about it. She hadn't felt the way she felt since she lived in New York and didn't know if she would bounce back this time around.

CHAPTER 24

It was a relief to be headed back home to Charlotte. Derek felt so accomplished once he left Dallas, he felt good about himself. Although he didn't know how the next few days would play out, he wasn't worried about it. He was confident that whatever happened would happen how it needed to. Derek was tired when he landed, but the messages that came through to his phone as he walked through the airport woke him up. He received several text messages from Preston about the art show, Katie's ex showing up, and Katie not being aware that Derek was out of town. Derek also looked on social media to see Katie's friends in the club twerking on camera, dancing, and drinking. Katie's ex-boyfriend Isaac also appeared in one of the videos from the club, causing millions of different scenarios to run through Derek's mind.

When he made it to his car, he immediately began driving towards Katie's place. His initial plan was to go see her the next day after her father Walter went to see her. But after what Derek saw, he wanted to get to Katie as soon as possible and see what was going on. It was rare for Katie to be up late, but with her friends in town, Derek wasn't sure what the case would be. As Derek drove, he also began to feel stupid considering that he and Katie hadn't spoken almost the entire week.

A car was going through the community gates when Derek pulled in, so he drove right in behind them before the gates closed. He saw Katie's Jeep parked and pulled into the space right next to it. Derek wanted to call her prior to showing up to her place but couldn't pull himself to do so. After some slight hesitation, Derek knocked on the door a few times. No one answered, causing Derek's mind to wander even more. He started to wonder if Katie was out at the club with her friends, which led to him picturing her standing in a section with her ex-boyfriend or out dancing on the dance floor with him. All the thoughts began to make Derek a little anxious, visualizing what a confrontation between him and Isaac would look like. He then shook his head, stopping himself from even entertaining it. Derek walked back to the parking lot, heart beating fast. He hated the fact that he felt nervous.

"You lost?"

Derek turned around to see Katie and Bianca both standing there, staring at him. The two of them held white paper bags and cups from a burger spot that wasn't far away. The sweats and flip flops that they both wore let Derek know that they hadn't been out anywhere. They both had their hair in a bun and no make-up on their faces.

"Back from your trip?" Bianca asked as she walked past him and up the stairs.

Despite the innocent look on Bianca's face, her sarcasm was obvious.

"She never misses the chance to take shots at me," Derek said to Katie.

Katie simply raised her eyebrows as she began to walk past Derek, not responding.

"Really? That's what we on?" Derek softly grabbed Katie's arm.

Katie immediately snatched her arm away.

"Excuse me? You haven't talked to me all week so what's different now? That's what we *been* on, clearly."

"I texted you, you didn't respond to me," Derek defended himself.

Katie's face went from a frown to a blank stare.

"You have to be freaking kidding me." She turned to fully face Derek. "You texted me this morning and that was enough right? That's you talking to me this week?"

"I mean... that's technically this week though," Derek said with a smirk on his face.

He tried to lighten the tension, but it was not effective at all. Katie began to walk away once again, fuming. Derek stepped in front of her, attempting to calm her down.

"It's not like I heard from you either," Derek said. "It wasn't just me."

"If we about to play the blame game, we can just go back to not speaking. Forget it."

"We can't talk? I'm not trying to stand out here and argue with you."

"We couldn't talk this whole week? You disappeared, gave me a silent treatment. A silent treatment. That is weak, weak! I told you, I don't like that. We don't solve problems like that," Katie got in his face.

"We don't need to make a scene. Chill," Derek said to her quietly as he looked around the parking lot.

An older white woman walking her dog continued to glance over at Derek and Katie.

"I hear you. I could have reached out sooner. At this point, I'm tired of fighting, I came over here—"

"Why?" Katie cut him off. "Why? You thought I was over it since you didn't hear from me? You over here to make sure I haven't washed my hands of you?"

"STOP," Derek said strongly. "I'm right here trying to tell you that you are right. I'm trying to end all of it and put it behind us."

Katie began to respond but stopped herself, looking away. Derek began to feel worse, realizing that Katie wasn't in the best place.

"I didn't come over here to talk about who did what," Derek said. "I'm really over here because I love you."

Katie scoffed and rolled her eyes, turning her back on Derek.

"I'm serious," Derek got in front of her.

Katie still refused to look at him.

"It was a lot when we got back, and it wasn't cool closing you out all week and not being there for you. I own up to that, not denying it, and I'm saying I'm sorry for it."

Katie still didn't respond, looking off into the distance. She began to wipe her eyes as a tear finally began to roll down her cheek.

"Most of my life, I've been used to keeping it pushing, not getting too attached because it keeps you from getting disappointed. It's how I came up; friends, women, all that. I'm not saying it's right; it's just the truth. You challenge that part of me. I always knew I wanted you and once I got you, I already had this idea of you in my head. That first few months you were in New York, there was only so much either of us could see, so my guards were down. But you know, the longer we were together, the more I learned the real you and vice versa. I was used to just falling all the way back whenever I saw something I didn't like. It's hard to get out of that way of thinking, I still struggle with it and that's real. I'm not trying to fall back or let us lose what we have."

Katie's phone suddenly began to ring, she looked to see that Bianca was calling and declined the call.

"I just want us to be good," Derek continued.

Katie let out a loud sigh.

"Why do you keep thinking you gotta' protect yourself from me? It's not even just you; men in general do this. People act like they have to get you before you get them, even if y'all are together. I'm putting myself out there just as much as you are, open to get hurt just like you are. I'm not just looking out for me; I'm looking out for you too. I don't have any hidden agendas. If you thought I was a well put together, flawless person, you are going to keep being disappointed. I have issues as does my family as you can see. I have areas that need work just like you do. We are two imperfect people and never will be perfect."

Katie's phone began to ring, Bianca was calling once again.

"I'm good B, I'm cool," Katie said when she answered.

Bianca then said something that made Katie chuckle before she hung up. Derek felt a slight sense of relief seeing a grin out of Katie.

"Look, the whole thing at the lake house was just... a lot, that was—"

"I'm not even on that," Derek interrupted. "It is what it is. I just want us to be good."

Katie was slightly surprised but didn't contest.

"How did you even know I was here?" Katie asked. "I might have been at the club."

Derek gave her a skeptical look, causing her to smile.

"Please, yeah right," Derek said.

"You pulled up to make sure Isaac was nowhere around, I know your friends told you he was at the art show, didn't they?" Katie asked. "You wanted to make sure he wasn't around me."

Derek nodded as he couldn't hold his smile back.

"So predictable!" Katie yelled, a full smile on her face. "But there is nothing. He was there, and he spoke to me just so you know. Do you want to know what about?"

Derek didn't respond. He also didn't want to look as if he didn't trust her or was insecure. Derek then stepped a little closer to Katie, a somewhat nervous look on his face.

"Was I your safe choice?" Derek asked.

"My what?"

"You know, a safe choice. After all that time, all the years of knowing me, you gave me a chance finally. I'm asking if it's because I was a safe choice. You know, the nice guy, reliable. The last resort you could bank on."

Katie put her head down, making Derek uncomfortable. She then looked up at him.

"No," she simply said. "Did you not just explain to me your commitment issues and ability to ghost on me at any moment?"

"Like that?" Derek asked as they both laughed.

"There's no such thing as a safe choice. There's a smart choice, and when I got smarter, I made a better choice. Nothing feels fully safe about being vulnerable with someone. We build trust, in time. I'm not here just because I *think* you're a good man, I've seen it in how you've always treated me even when you weren't with me. I'm not desperate for a safe choice, I chose who I wanted."

Derek reached out and pulled Katie close to him, giving her a long hug.

"Don't listen to anything my dad said," Katie said as they hugged. "I'm done with him, done letting him have a hold on my life."

Derek put his arm around her as he walked her toward her apartment door.

"I'm just glad you don't look like him," Derek said to her.

Katie let out a laugh.

"Yes, we thank God for that!"

Through the laughs and smiles, Derek hoped that Katie wasn't so far gone that his trip to Dallas ended up being in vain.

CHAPTER 25

Friday evening turned out to set the tone for how the following morning would be, somewhat of a roller coaster. Katie went to the gym Saturday morning to get back into her routine. While there, her mom called to talk about how Jared got in a small car accident that morning. Thankfully, it wasn't anything major, but enough for him to be a little shaken up. Despite making amends with Paris and Imani that morning before they went to the airport, she could tell that there was still hostility. Sabrina informed Katie that there was a moment the night before where Paris cried in the nightclub they went to, then bounced back and downplayed it. They all wanted to chalk it up to alcohol, but Katie knew better. She knew she spoke the truth the night before and didn't regret any of it. Her morning was a little up and down, but she felt it could have been worse.

Katie was most relieved that she and Derek made amends. As angry as she was before, it couldn't compare to the relief she felt. Katie felt bad about Derek being caught in the crossfires of her family issues. At the same time, she felt a sense of relief as if all pressure and weight was lifted from her shoulders. In her mind, she was back to square one, how life was previously. She found a slight sense of peace in the fact that she extended the olive branch and tried to amend things. Even with the slight sense of peace, she couldn't help but to think a lot about how things were when she was younger living in Houston.

Most of Katie's day was spent at the church, working with the other members of the hospitality team on decorations and preparing for Sunday. While Katie knew a lot of the other women from church, she rarely spent time with them outside of church. They invited her places and made attempts to connect with her many times, but she would rarely go. She often wanted to be left alone. Her conversations with them as they worked on setting up for Sunday began to make her regret not spending more time with them. Two of them were the same age as Katie while the others were a few years older. There were only two men in hospitality, and they were in their late thirties.

When Sunday arrived, everything was well laid out and decorated. Visitors were welcomed by several greeters when they walked in and offered refreshments. Katie communicated by text message with Tasha most of the morning, keeping her up to date. Tasha was away with her husband, visiting family, so she wouldn't be there. Katie sent her pictures of the decorations and the layout, Tasha loved it and continued to praise Katie's efforts along with everyone else's. The sanctuary began to fill up quickly, many members from the sister church came in and began to talk and fellowship in the lobby. Katie hadn't smiled as much as she did in a while. She was even more excited when Miah walked in with her son Deron. The weekend made Katie appreciate Miah's friendship even more and made her want to spend even more time with her. There was never jealousy, envy, or hidden motives with Miah, which was something Katie appreciated. She was also glad that Miah came because of all that she'd dealt with the previous week with Deron's father being killed. Miah had to continually deal with people asking her how she felt about it and was tired of discussing it.

"It's so many people here…stop Deron," Miah stopped Deron from jumping around.

"Yeah, our sister church is here so it's more packed than usual," Katie said.

"Did you see all those dudes on the corner outside?" Miah asked.

"Who?"

Miah pointed as others also began to walk in mentioning some people outside being disruptive. Katie walked outside to the parking lot out of curiosity. In the distance, she could see a large group of black men all dressed alike, two of them were standing on a bench preaching through a bullhorn. The two of them spoke aggressively, trying to provoke those who walked past, talking about God, racism, and about how they were the true chosen people.

"I don't know what they got going on," Katie said as she, Miah, and Deron walked back into the building behind a few others.

"How was the art show and all that?" Miah asked sarcastically.

"It was nice," Katie said. "The weekend overall was a little trash, but… you know."

"Oh, you know I know," Miah's eyebrows raised. "I'm sure we'll talk about it."

When Miah and Deron went to find their seats, Katie peaked her head in to see that service was filling up fast. Katie just hoped that Pastor Loren didn't dig too much into the shooting that happened, for Miah's sake. Traffic in the foyer began to slow down. Katie along with the rest of the team were able to get a little breather. When Katie heard the music begin, she began to move her fingers, imitating Derek playing on the keyboard. Pastor Loren's wife, Carla, then emerged from the sanctuary into the lobby. She always had a presence about her because of her large smile and because she was one of the best dressed women in the church. Carla began to hug and commend everyone for the job that they'd done, she was one of the sweetest women that a person would meet in the world.

"Everything is beautiful. We are going to dinner this week. This is just...wow," she said to Katie and a few of the others.

Carla then turned around when she noticed someone who looked lost.

"Hi! You looking for where to go? Confusing, I know!" Carla laughed.

Carla tapped Katie on the shoulder, whose back was turned as she talked to the others.

"Honey, can you get him a program and see if he wants any food?" Carla said.

Katie turned around and froze as if she'd seen a ghost. Her phone fell out of her hand and hit the floor. As she stood frozen, her father Walter stood towering over her.

CHAPTER 26

Charlotte was a city Walter hadn't seen in years, which was surprising considering how much he traveled for business purposes. His trip was delayed by a day due to his son Jared getting into a car accident. Walter was just thankful that Jared was okay and the damages to his car were not major. Even more so than not having been to Charlotte, Walter hadn't stepped foot in a church since he was a young teenager. He was more skeptical than most when it came to church and especially when it came to preachers. Although he wasn't the most spiritual, he'd never sent up as many small prayers as he did that morning. Derek texted him most of the morning to let him know where the church was and what time to be there. Church gave Walter an uneasy feeling because he always associated it with his first experience inside of one, which was a funeral. Church also reminded Walter of his father, who dragged him, Jeffrey, and Janice to church every Sunday but was one of the biggest monsters in Walter's eyes.

Walter didn't anticipate seeing his daughter as soon as he walked in. Katie's facial expression of surprise was one that he could live with, much better than what he expected. No words were exchanged between the two of them; Katie walked away when she saw him. One of the other women provided him with a welcome program and offered him refreshments while the other picked Katie's phone up off the floor. Walter declined and was then escorted into the sanctuary, not attempting to follow Katie.

During the service, Walter found himself observing and mentally critiquing more than paying attention. He was impressed by Derek's ability to play the keyboard and other instruments. Walter also continued to glance back at the doors to see if Katie had come in. While he didn't see Katie, he continued to catch some of the women from the lobby peaking their heads in every few minutes. Every time Walter caught them looking, they'd quickly look away or back out of the door. Katie, accompanied by a few others, eventually walked in. They all walked hastily towards a certain section of seating, which let Walter know that the ones peaking their heads in were doing so to locate him. The pastor, Roy Loren, then appeared in front of the congregation, beginning to preach after the announcements were made. Roy caught Walter's attention with the way that he spoke. He didn't have the theatrical dramatics or prolonged wording that Walter expected, Roy spoke clearly and directly. Walter found himself more engaged in the message than he wanted to be.

"You feel like you have the right to hold people's faults over their heads yet walk in here and expect God to overlook yours. Who do you think you are? You better than God? God shows mercy but you think you're too good to do so? Who are you?" Roy asked rhetorically as the congregation reacted. "Then some of you feel like you are God's gift to everyone in your life and that you are flawless. Surely you aren't the problem! It MUST be them. I ask again, who do you think you are?"

While some in the congregation yelled and applauded Roy, others wrestled with his words.

"Money, accolades, and favors don't make up for you being unbearable and toxic, I know people that would do a lot for me that I can't spend five minutes with...because they feel that they are entitled to treat people any way they want to."

Walter didn't go up for prayer at the end of service, but rather went out to the parking lot as others began to exit. He felt more comfortable outside, avoiding the awkwardness of forced smiles and stiff conversations with people. Walter knew it would be almost impossible to pinpoint Katie with so many people around. Derek suddenly rushed outside and began to jog towards the side of the building, causing Walter to quickly walk in the same direction. When he rounded the corner, the parking lot on the side of the church came into view. Katie's jeep was parked there along with a few other cars, Derek and Katie stood in front of her Jeep going back and forth.

"I need to go. Can you give me my keys please?" Katie repeated frantically.

Whenever Derek would try to talk, Katie would continue to talk over him and repeat herself. Derek glanced up to see Walter walking towards them.

"Your keys are in my bag inside," Derek told her, causing Katie to let out a frustrated sigh and hang her head.

"Why would you…" she rolled her eyes. "Can you go—"

"I'm going," Derek said, frustrated.

He quickly walked through the side doors that Katie left out of. Katie kept her back turned as she acknowledged people that were leaving, bidding them farewell and safe travels home. She then began to eagerly scroll and text on her phone. Walter walked over and stood in front of her. When Katie attempted to make a phone call, Walter grabbed the phone and pulled it out of Katie's hands.

"I won't be long," Walter said. "Just hear me and I'll be on my way."

"What is taking so long to grab my keys?" Katie paced back and forth, ignoring Walter.

Walter bit his tongue and simply nodded.

"Never mind, maybe it's too soon. Don't worry about it, I'll leave you to it."

Walter turned and began to walk back towards the front parking lot.

"What are you even doing here?" Katie suddenly asked.

"I came here to see you."

"To see me? You came here solely to see me?"

"Yes," Walter said, walking back towards her.

Walter could see that Katie had no intention of making reconciliation with her easy, and he had to fight to keep his composure.

"I'm sure I'm the last person you want to see, and I'll take that. I'm not giving you a long speech or something dramatic. I'm here because I want this feud between the two of us to be over."

Katie's facial expression did not change; she maintained a straight emotionless face that Walter was often known for. Nothing that Walter said moved her.

"I was wrong in a lot of areas and I want to start over," Walter said.

"Start over? Just like that?" Katie asked, hostile. "It's that easy in your mind?"

"Why isn't it?"

Katie slowly walked towards Walter.

"You don't get it. You don't understand how these last few years have taken a toll on me. I hated you. I came out of a dark place and made my mind up years ago that I wasn't going to cry over this or lose sleep over it anymore. Last weekend set me back. I don't want to deal with this anymore, it's too much. You thought coming here was going to make everything okay? Is that what you hoped for?"

"What are you saying? That you want nothing to do with me? You sound as if you want to keep it the way it has been."

Katie stared at Walter, not responding.

"I haven't been the best father to you, I know. My focus got off; my priorities got mixed up. I lost sight of what is important, and I get it now. We can fix this."

"I don't see it being that easy," Katie wiped her eyes.

"It won't be. I'm asking you to work with me," Walter said.

Walter realized how much he'd drifted away from his daughter as he stared at her. It hadn't hit him until he stood across from her and began to feel heavy.

He began to remember so many memories of Katie's childhood, causing the conversation to become even more difficult for him. Walter once again felt the discomfort of vulnerability and exposure that he felt during service.

"I love you," Walter said, something he hadn't said in a long time.

Katie didn't respond to him, which made Walter begin to feel that his relationship with his daughter was gone for good. Derek then reappeared, slowly walking out of the doors with Katie's keys in his hand. She quickly walked toward him with her hand extended for the keys. Derek pulled his hand back, keeping her from grabbing her keys.

"Are you really about to do this?" Derek asked her.

Katie's eyes widened, feeling a slight sense of betrayal. She scuffled over close to Derek, making it difficult for Walter to hear anything that the two of them were saying to one another. As he watched the two of them from a distance, he began to remember all the times he had to cheer Katie up or calm her down when she was young. Walter didn't understand why so many memories began to hit him at once, but each memory made his heart heavier. When Katie saw Walter struggle to keep his composure and show sorrow, her eyes locked in on him. Walter quickly turned his back towards then, attempting to quickly get himself together. After a few minutes, he felt a hand tug on his shoulder. He didn't want to turn around, but the hand continued to tug harder and harder. By the time Walter turned around, quite a few tears had rolled down his face. Katie marveled at the tears on Walter's face as she stood in front of him. Katie then reached both of her arms out and gave her father a strong hug, beginning to cry. Derek stood back in the distance close to the door with a grin on his face, arms crossed. Troy quietly walked out of the doors, standing next to Derek as he watched Walter and Katie hug. Troy was amazed at what he saw, shaking Derek's hand.

"You that dude," Troy said, "putting families back together."

"Nah man, that's all God," Derek said to him. "God did this."

CHAPTER 27

Isaac Duke cruised through the city of Charlotte Sunday evening, enjoying the rental car that he would have until the next morning. He listened to a woman ramble to him on the phone about her day and other random topics. Isaac enjoyed seeing some old friends over the weekend and hanging in some of his old spots but would feel even better about his entire weekend if his evening played out the way he wanted it to. He felt good about himself, and the cologne he had on along with the clothes he'd put on at his hotel made him feel even better.

Earlier that day after leaving a brunch, and after a few mimosas, Isaac sent a text as a last-ditch effort to recapture who he felt was always his, Katie Berry. People always preached that the past was something that could not be changed, but in Isaac's mind, some parts of it were worth trying to. Isaac told Katie that he just wanted to grab food and catch up before he left town, very modest and innocent despite having other intentions. Seeing Katie at the art show Friday night made Isaac even more determined to work his way back into her life. She was even more attractive than she was the last time he saw her. Isaac would be lying if he said physical attraction didn't play a part in him being anxious to be in the same space with her. He would be lying if he said he didn't have sleeping with her on his mind. He also felt a sense of urgency because it was no longer as easy to get a response from her as it used to be. Isaac didn't understand why Katie suddenly became hostile toward him, which is why he was quick to hop on the opportunity when she responded to him earlier telling him to come by.

Isaac also felt he had an ace in his back pocket, the rapport that he had with Katie's father over the years. Isaac and Walter saw the world through the same lenses in many ways. Walter respected Isaac's aggressive attitude and hustle toward success. Isaac was the type that went after what he wanted and kept after it until he got it. When Katie got into her new relationship, Isaac's confidence that he was safe became even stronger to many of his friends' surprise. To him, Katie's boyfriend Derek was weak, he and his entire group of friends, a group of guys that wanted to be something they weren't. Isaac didn't see a roadblock when he saw Derek, he saw a last resort that Katie settled on. In Isaac's mind, it would only be a matter of time before Derek would be out of the picture, and that time had come. Some people considered it dirty that he used to mention Derek to Walter's father, framing it as concern for her well-being and that she may be taking care of a man as opposed to being taken care of, but he didn't care. The woman on the car radio was still speaking to him, he hadn't listened to one word that she said.

"Babe, what are you about to do?" she asked, catching Isaac's attention.

"I'm just about to link up with a few of my boys before I leave tomorrow." Isaac turned onto the street where Katie's apartment was.

Once Isaac pulled up and parked, he got off the phone and pulled his shades off to look at himself in the mirror. He put some oil on his beard to make it shine, wore a tighter black shirt to show off his muscles and arms, and wore what used to be Katie's favorite cologne on him. He also wore the Rolex that Walter bought for him some years back. Isaac knew that Katie lived with her cousin Bianca, he looked for her car hoping that she wasn't home. He was still on good terms with some of Katie's friends, which was how he kept up with her life apart from social media. Bianca was someone that he was not on speaking terms with and didn't want her to run interference. Katie swung the front door open after Isaac knocked twice.

"Hey!" Katie smiled, looking Isaac up and down briefly.

"Hey, looking good as usual," Isaac said and smiled back.

"Thanks, come in," Katie stepped aside.

Isaac walked in, excited. The smell of garlic chicken hit his nostrils. He continued to look Katie up and down as she walked in front of him. Black tank top, grey sweats, bare foot; Isaac couldn't stop looking.

"There he is, look at him."

Isaac stopped in his tracks, caught off guard to see Walter sitting on the couch.

"Old man!" Isaac walked over, greeting him with a handshake and a hug.

Isaac tried to hide his look of surprise as he spoke with Walter. His mindset quickly switched when he saw that Walter was there, sounding much more respectful and innocent.

Is she serious right now? Isaac thought to himself. *Yeah she on some BS.*

"What you got?" Walter grabbed the bottle of wine in Isaac's hand. "Oh, you brought the good wine, the real wine."

"Katie didn't tell me you were in town, we could have planned something," Isaac said.

"Yeah it was a last-minute trip, came to see little Marie over there," Walter caused Katie to roll her eyes at hearing her middle name.

Isaac glanced in the kitchen to see Katie washing out a pot in the sink, not paying attention to him and Walter. Isaac felt more and more uncomfortable as time went on, he also began to feel more frustrated. His frustration was rooted in the fact that getting lucky before leaving Charlotte was out of the question.

"We can open this right now. Well, I guess us three. Buddy doesn't drink right?" Walter asked Katie.

"Not anymore," Katie said, still focused on the pot she was washing.

The sudden sound of a toilet flushing caught Isaac's attention.

"Thought he fell in back there," Katie said after hearing the toilet flush.

When Isaac glanced towards Katie's room, his face instantly felt hot. He didn't know what to do as Derek emerged from Katie's room, having used her bathroom.

"I thought he fell in," Walter purposely said so Derek could hear him.

Isaac maintained the fixed smile on his face, not sure what to do.

Is she serious? She really moving like this? Nah man.

"Those burritos from earlier got me," Derek smiled as he walked toward Walter.

"Told you about eating all those beans. Whoa back up now!" Walter put his hand to Derek's chest, stopping him from coming any closer. "Don't bring that gas over here."

"Alright, you remember last time you pushed me," Derek said, pointing at Walter.

"That is not funny!" Katie yelled as Walter and Derek both laughed.

Isaac felt humiliated. A huge smile came across Katie's face as Derek entered the kitchen to help her take the lasagna out of the oven. Katie hadn't looked in Isaac's direction once apart from when she opened the door for him.

"So, how are things?" Walter grabbed Isaac's attention. "I know you wanted to catch up in Dallas."

Isaac's thoughts were everywhere, he wanted to leave as fast as he could without embarrassing himself. He looked back into the kitchen once again to see Katie, still with a huge smile on her face, watch Derek cut the lasagna as they talked back and forth. Isaac pulled out his phone and went to his text messages although he had none.

"I just realized I have an important client presentation tomorrow; I just thought about it. Sorry about that, I really need to go prepare."

"What?" Walter frowned. "You just got here, you sure?"

"Yeah for sure," Isaac said.

There was no enthusiasm in his voice, he just wanted to get away immediately. Isaac felt deflated, a complete one eighty from how he felt when he pulled up.

"Yeah I understand," Walter said as he walked Isaac to the door.

Isaac didn't care to say anything to Katie. If she tried to say anything to him, he felt that he would have went off.

"You know that's a big part of life man, knowing when you should stick around and when you need to go," Walter said firmly, eyes fixed on Isaac.

Isaac nodded and shook Walter's hand.

"Oh, this is yours." Walter handed Isaac his bottle of wine, then pat him on the back as he walked out.

The door closed as soon as he walked out of it. The message was loud and clear.

CHAPTER 28

Two Months Later…

Charlotte, NORTH CAROLINA

The sun often made sure it was bright and shining for Sunday mornings. The congregation at GGC was coming down from their emotional high from praise and worship. Members were making their way back to their seats after hugging and greeting everyone. The praise team as well as the musicians were headed to their seats as well as Pastor Loren walked up to the podium, grabbing his tablet from his son Troy. He spoke softly and monotone, a little tired having just returned from Arizona the night before.

"Before anything, I need you all to join me in congratulating two of our own. Brother Derek and sister Katie got engaged last night," Pastor Loren smiled as the congregation roared with applause and excitement. "Y'all stand up for me, come on."

Derek slowly stood up and waived, blushing from the attention. Joy sat next to him with a huge smile on her face, waving her hand in the air dramatically, imitating praise and worship. Tasha walked over from her seat and gave Derek a big hug.

"Congratulations honey!" Tasha yelled in his ear over the congregation's applause and shouts.

Derek turned around to see Katie standing in her usual section, also blushing. Derek's mother Gloria sat beside Katie, clapping with a beaming smile on her face.

"So awesome. Always a blessing when young people come together," Pastor Loren said as the congregation cosigned with a resounding 'Amen'. "Both of them, very beautiful people. It's hard these days to just find legitimately good people. With these two, it seems like it was just a match made in heaven, easy, no major problems, seems like it was smooth."

The congregation laughed as Derek and Katie both turned and looked at each other, eyebrows raised.

"Look at them, they lookin' like 'Pastor if only you knew!'" Pastor Loren made the whole church burst out into laughter again.

After service, Derek walked with his mother Gloria towards his car. Gloria came into town the day before to be there for the proposal.

"Did your dad call you?" Gloria asked.

"Yeah this morning, said Val showed him the pictures," Derek said.

"Oh nice, she saw them on whatever that app is y'all be on?" Gloria asked.

"No, I sent them to her," Derek said, chuckling.

"What? A lot of people were recording last night, and you know y'all put everything online now," Gloria said. "I just had to ask."

When Gloria sat in the passenger seat of the car, she looked behind Derek.

"Aren't you going to go say something to your fiancé before we go?"

Derek turned around to see Katie in her Jeep, parked, looking down at her phone. Derek then looked back at his mother.

"Go on now," Gloria shewed him away. "Don't act bashful now."

Gloria pulled out her ringing phone and began to talk to one of her friends about Derek's proposal. Derek walked over to the driver side window of Katie's Jeep. While Katie was typing a text, Derek couldn't help but to stare at the engagement ring on her finger. It made him feel good to see it, and hearing people comment and brag on it made him stick his chest out even more.

"Dinner tonight?" Katie interrupted his thoughts. "You, me, and your mom."

"Let's do it."

"My parents hate that they missed it last night, I've been texting them all morning. My mom is finally starting to feel better," Katie said, throwing her phone onto the passenger seat. "They'll be here next weekend though, hope you're ready."

"Right, hope they like me," Derek took a deep breath in sarcasm, leaning on the driver side door.

"I don't know. You think you'll be ready?" Katie turned in her seat towards him.

"I hope so, gotta' pray," Derek nodded.

"Yup," Katie also nodded.

"Yup," Derek echoed.

They kept a straight face as long as they could, then burst out laughing.

"I am glad all of that is over," Derek said.

"Who are you telling?" Katie leaned back. "That was a lot."

"How are you and your dad?" Derek asked.

"We're working on it, getting there. Some stuff just takes time you know?"

Derek nodded. Katie forgave Walter and there were no issues between the two of them, but to fully open back up to him again took much more time than she thought it would.

"I still can't believe you went back there to talk to him," Katie said as she put her hand on top of Derek's. "I'm still like…in awe."

"I had to do what I had to do."

"You really trying to be the one huh?" Katie asked.

"Here you go," Derek sighed.

"You really trying to be like that with the girl huh?" Katie continued.

"Woman if you don't go on," he made her laugh.

Katie pulled off, waving at Gloria. Derek watched as Katie drove off.

"That's what kind of man I am."

CHAPTER 29

Dallas, TEXAS

Mondays always had the reputation of being stressful and undesirable. Walter usually didn't buy into that way of thinking, but this Monday was a day that wore him out. Mondays for Walter consisted of back-to-back meetings, tedious reporting and forecast calls. He'd also been taking care of Laura, who was sick for the last few days, while staying on top of his work. They both were a bit sour that they weren't able to make it to see their daughter get engaged, but Walter wanted Laura to put her health first. He was finally beginning to develop a proper work-life balance in the last two months, making a conscious effort to keep the two separate. Despite a few moments where he bumped heads with Whitney, the acting CFO, he didn't allow it to knock him off course. Walter sat back from his computer and tossed his glasses onto his desk. He was tired of looking at his computer and didn't want to look at another spread sheet or report. His phone began to ring, his wife Laura's picture flashed across the screen.

"Yes ma'am," Walter answered.

"What time is your meeting today?" Laura asked.

"In about ten. Should be short," Walter looked at the calendar invite on his computer. "Yeah, it's only set for fifteen minutes."

"What do you think it's about?" Laura's question caused Walter to frown.

"I don't know, I haven't really thought about it," Walter chuckled. "Why?"

"I mean, just asking."

Though she sounded relaxed, Walter knew her better than that. Over the last month, there were several layoffs in the company and even some major players lost their jobs, so Walter was sure that Laura was uneasy.

"Everything will be fine. It's nothing to be uneasy about," Walter told her.

"Well, make sure you're set to be off Friday so we can go to Charlotte. We need to pick up Katie's engagement gift too, I'm definitely not sending that in the mail."

"Engagement gift?" Walter began to pack his bag.

"We talked about this, JR," Laura sighed. "Remember what I showed you?"

"Yes, yes," Walter said, although he completely forgot but was sure that his wife chose something that would cost a hefty price.

He began walking towards Matthias' office while continuing to listen to Laura ramble for the rest of the conversation. As Walter walked down the hall, he couldn't help but to notice the facilities crew cleaning out some offices that were now vacant.

"I'll just talk to you when you get home," Laura said before hanging up.

Walter got to Matthias' office and was immediately signaled to enter in. He hadn't spoken to Matthias much since their last meeting two months prior. Over the last two months, Walter sought to stay out the spotlight and stay out of the way. Matthias moved from Los Angeles to Dallas shortly after he told Walter that he would not be getting promoted, but he continued to travel back and forth because he was in love with Los Angeles.

"How's it going?" Matthias shook Walter's hand. "It's been quite a while."

"Yeah, it has been."

"Follow me," Matthias said before Walter could sit down.

The two of them walked into the same executive conference room that the two of them went to when they last spoke. Matthias didn't waste time.

"I wanted to bring you in just to cut down on the speculation. You've seen quite a few people getting walked out of here the last few weeks, quite a few that you've worked alongside at one moment in time. As you also know, we've done quite a bit of realignment around here. The goal is to do what is best for everyone, that's always what I aim to do."

Walter nodded, not showing too much. He wasn't sure where Matthias was going and didn't care too much. He was just ready to get home and wanted Matthias to get to the point.

"After two months of investigation, we found several leaks. Most of those who have been led out of here were found to be accomplices in the matter," Matthias said, causing Walter's eyes to widen. "We have now cut the head of the snake."

Matthias threw two pictures onto the table, causing Walter's mouth to drop. The pictures were of Whitney meeting with some people, the passing of envelopes, and overall very questionable photos.

"Crazy, isn't it?" Matthias quickly picked up the photos. "Right under our noses. Me and some others have had our eyes on him for some time. It was heavily against my father's wishes, but the purpose of me putting him in that CFO seat was to give him enough rope to hang himself. He got sloppy because he got elevated, just as I'd hoped. Two months gave the investigators all that they needed, so it's time to move on."

Walter was surprised, but felt no sympathy being that he was overlooked. A part of him even enjoyed hearing what he was hearing. In his mind, Matthias and the rest of the board had brought it on themselves.

"I filled you in on all of that to say, none of it had anything to do with your abilities or lack thereof. I know there was a bit of friction two months ago, but the less people involved in a situation like this, the better," Matthias said.

Walter began to feel a little remorse about all the things he said and thought over the last two months. It also made him feel foolish for how he acted with his family.

"So, I say all of that to say, the company will need a CFO to be officially effective next month. The seat is yours for the taking, are you in?" Matthias asked bluntly.

Walter didn't expect to be offered a seat at the table. Two months prior, Walter would have accepted with no questions asked. Currently, being offered a seat at the high table didn't sound as appealing as it once did.

"The board loves you, and I got in many good graces again once I informed them," Matthias smiled, finally getting a grin out of Walter.

"Wow," Walter said. "I honestly felt that this just wasn't for me, and that I wasn't working hard enough."

"It never was that. Sometimes things don't come at the time we want them to, but when they do, they're that much sweeter. Things come together in time," Matthias said to him. "Do what you will with that."

Walter let out a small laugh as Matthias pat him on the back.

"I just need to discuss it with my family," Walter said. "When do you need to know?"

"Take your time," Matthias told him. "I get I just dumped a lot on you."

"I just want to discuss it with them before deciding. It's a big step."

"Yes, it is," Matthias said to him. "Fair enough. Go, talk to your *family*. But one more thing, thank you for staying diligent even during all of this."

Matthias walked out of the conference room, leaving Walter behind, who stood there processing what he was just offered. Even with the offer now being there for him to take, all Walter could think about was his family and getting home to them.

CHAPTER 30

Walter's drive home was one of the most relaxed he had had in a long time. It still hadn't hit him yet that the move he'd been waiting for had finally come; but he wasn't as anxious about it as he thought he would be two months ago. Walter drove his usual way home, pulling into his neighborhood around the usual time he always did.

When he walked in the house, the smell of dinner hit his nostrils as it usually did. The sound of a loud crash and glass shattering came from upstairs, grabbing his attention. When his daughter Olivia ran to the stairs to go down them, she froze when she saw Walter standing by the front door.

"What did you do?" Walter asked her calmly.

Laura then appeared out of the kitchen, immediately looking up at Olivia at the top of the stairs. She didn't say anything, just stared, which caused Olivia to begin to squirm. Tristan appeared behind Olivia, also with an innocent confused look on his face.

"I will deal with the both of you when I'm done," Laura said, not raising her voice.

Laura then looked at Walter and shook her head.

"We just couldn't be done after the first two, could we?"

"Hey now, you—"

"Ahh whatever," Laura waved him off as he put his arm around her.

Laura was anxious to hear about what happened at the job, something that she didn't mind as of late because Walter wasn't bitter about it like he used to be. Walter explained to her all that happened and casually mentioned that he was offered the role of Chief Financial Officer of the company. Laura was more ecstatic than Walter was.

"I thought you would be bouncing off the walls. This is what you've been waiting for!"

"Yeah," Walter said with a shrug. "It's a great opportunity for sure, I'm just not as pressed as I was. I'm…good. I'm okay right now."

Laura's eyes widened, and she held the back of her hand up to his forehead to check him for a fever.

"Did I get you sick? Do you have the flu? Some type of contagion?"

Walter laughed.

"No, I'm not sick," Walter said as he pulled Laura close to him.

"I just changed where I was putting my time and energy. When I look back, I was just diving into work to keep from having to think about all the issues with the family. You know what, no, I know that's what I was doing. All of the stuff with Janice, Katie, everything, but now that everything is coming around, I'm good."

Laura smiled and laid her forehead against Walter's.

"I prayed for this day, my goodness," she said.

Walter's phone began to vibrate, they both looked at the phone to see Walter's brother Jeffrey was calling. Laura sighed then stood up. She gave Walter a quick peck on the cheek before heading back into the kitchen. Walter grabbed his phone and headed towards his office.

"Thought you weren't gonna' answer the phone; you know how you do," Jeffrey said.

"Shut up," Walter said.

Walter sat in the firm leather chair behind his desk.

"Crazy about Whitney, huh?" Jeffrey asked.

"How do you know about that?"

"I hear everything. A little birdie told me that he got picked up by the authorities tonight. He was based in Boston, remember? Always been shady," Jeffrey said. "That's why I told you not to worry about it, it was only a matter of time."

"Yes, you did," Walter conceded. "I should have listened. I'll give you that."

"As usual, me being right and you having to catch up," Jeffrey sighed.

"Are you finished?"

"You know I have to give you a hard time."

"My whole life!" Walter put his feet up on his desk.

"Janice has a business idea that she wants to run by us, a family business type of situation," Jeffrey said. "The three of us need to plan to meet up."

"She called me last night right after I got back and mentioned it. I told her I was open to hearing more. When and where?"

"And I can't believe that little Katie is engaged," Jeffrey completely switched lanes.

"Yeah she is," Walter smiled. "It's pretty surreal."

"I remember her running around playing with toys, trying to wear Laura's make up."

"They grow up fast. I can honestly say I'm proud of her. She is an amazing daughter."

"Yeah she's always been sharp," Jeffrey agreed. "And you're about to add another son to the tribe."

"That too," Walter let out a heavy sigh. "He's a good dude, I like him. I'm still getting to know him, but he's proven so far that he's the right one for her."

"Good, good," Jeffrey said.

His comment was followed by a long pause, which caught Walter's attention. Awkward silences with Jeffrey were rare.

"So, Janice is saying the best place for us to meet is in South Carolina," Jeffrey said hesitantly.

Walter immediately felt tightness in his stomach, and a slight feeling of anger toward Jeffrey stirred up inside of him.

"Now I know what you are thinking—"

"No, you don't. Of all places, you want to meet in South Carolina? For what?"

"Jonah Lee is sick."

There was another moment of silence on the phone.

"His wife called me this morning, said she's been calling everyone to come and see him. Me and Janice agreed we need to go; we haven't seen him in a long time."

"And that's thanks to who? That's not on us or anything we did," Walter said.

"JR, stop," Jeffrey said strongly. "At the end of the day, that's our daddy. We have to go, sort all these years of BS out and put it in the rearview. You got your daughter back JR, remember that."

Walter sighed and sat back in his chair, thinking. He began to feel the same heavy feeling he felt when he was in Charlotte with Katie. All that he had just experienced the past few months enabled him to have much more perspective.

"Okay," Walter simply said.

"Okay?" Jeffrey asked. "Okay what?"

"I'm going to Charlotte next week. I will drive to South Carolina from there. Meet me."

Jeffrey let out a sigh of relief.

"That won't be a problem, and I know this is hard. Janice and I are struggling with it too, which is why the three of us must go together. Like I told you before, nothing comes before the family, and we must keep the family together. We not about to let what happened to our generation happen again."

"I know Jeff," Walter agreed, looking at a picture that was sent to his phone earlier.

It was a picture sent to him by Derek. Derek was standing with his arm around Katie along with quite a few people in the distance behind them. Katie had her hand out towards the camera, showing her engagement ring. Her other hand was covering her mouth, giving a dramatic look of shock for the camera. A huge smile beamed across Walter's face.

"I know all too well."

END.

AUTHOR BIO

Darrius Williams is a young aspiring author born and raised in Milwaukee, Wisconsin. Discovering his love and niche for creative writing at the age of six, Darrius has a true passion for storytelling and creativity. Apart from writing as well as reading, he enjoys everything sports, working out, and spending time with his loved ones.